ARTISTS & THIEVES

A NOVEL BY

LINDA SCHROEDER

INDI PUBLISHING GROUP

ARIZONA

Artists & Thieves

This is a work of fiction. Names, characters, places, and incidents are products of the author's imagination or are used fictitiously. Any resemblance to actual events, locales, or persons living or dead is entirely coincidental.

13-Digit ISBN:978-1-935636-0-21

Library of Congress Control Number: 2010921470. I

INDI Publishing Group
www.writersreaders.com

Book design by Jackie Merri Meyer
http://web.me.com/jackie.meyer/MeyerNewYork/HOME.html

Illustration: iStockPhoto © Simon Oxley
Typography: Bembo and Beata

Printed in the United States

1 2 3 4 5 6 7 8 9 0
First Edition

ARTISTS & THIEVES

PROLOGUE

This story begins with another story. An ancient story. Ancient stories are always our beginnings. Come sit in the shade of this willow. My voice is old and I speak just loud enough for you to hear above the soft splashing of the river on those black rocks.

This tale is of an oracle's secret bowl and begins with a peacock's cry. A sharp cry from the top of a willow just like this one. A cry that tells us, if you know peacocks, nothing good ever comes of secrets.

It was more than twenty-five hundred years ago that the peacock cried in a Zhou Dynasty garden on a hot summer day. The youngest concubine of the king fanned herself as she sat by a latticed window high in the palace overlooking the garden and wished, no doubt, that she were permitted outside to feel a gentle breath of wind through the cinnamon scented cassia trees. Each time the iridescent blue neck of the peacock arched and its feather crown fluttered, she sighed along with its cry.

I imagine she was very beautiful, even in the heat.

The king's oracle, an old man, although not as old as I am, hurried across the tiles of the garden path. Sunlight shimmered off his golden robe and his quick steps glided silently beneath it. He carried oranges for a ritual offering.

Behind him, a court artist, a young man, generations younger than I am, kept pace with long steady strides. His red silk robe draped close against his body as if it were formed from the molten bronze of the palace foundry. The king's youngest concubine watched him walk beneath her latticed window. Suddenly, the peacock, in the way of fowl, swooped out of the willow directly in front of the artist. Naturally, the artist stumbled. He fell into the thick canes of bamboo which grew under the latticed window.

Of course, the king's youngest concubine laughed.

The artist blushed. What else could he do? She laughed again, this time more softly because she knew about the artist from court gossips and had not intended to embarrass him. To hide her laughter, she began to sing.

"Keep up," the oracle yelled as he continued by the pink peony bushes and white umbrella flowers of angelica of the inner compound of the palace, an area accessible only to important court officials. And the oracle was, indeed, very important, for he read the future in the patterns of yarrow stalks, predicted the success or failure of every event significant to the king. Would the hunt today yield food for the palace tables? Should a marriage contract be signed tomorrow? Could troops be moved within striking distance of enemy camps before autumn?

But in the heat of the day, the oracle did not have the artist in tow to answer questions for the king. No. He had a private reason.

The red tile roof and upturned eaves of the oracle's temple blazed with heat. "Wait over there," the oracle said to the artist, pointing to the stone bench under another willow. Only when the artist sat down did the oracle carefully slide open the temple's door. An ivory and jade screen blocked straight line access to the room. The screen prevented unbidden ghosts from turning into the ritual space, since ghosts, like dragons, could only travel in straight lines. Unfortunately, spies from the court, rivals for the oracle's position, were capable of turning.

I pause to tell you now, nothing good ever comes from spies.

Listen carefully.

The oracle turned sharply right. He saw no spy. After he poured wine sweetened with cassia bark into a ritual bowl, he set it with the oranges on a table as an offering to the king's ancestors. Then he lifted a bronze octagonal vessel from a chest. Sweat dripped from his face and the vessel nearly slipped from his damp hands.

On each of the vessel's eight sides were trigrams, three lines formed of either broken or unbroken segments, yin/yang symbols that were ancient even then. Within the vessel were fifty yarrow stalks. Although he was hot and extremely nervous, the oracle patiently placed the fifty yarrow stalks on the table and divided and regrouped them again and again, until he had, by the chance of the groupings, a numeric sequence corresponding to two trigrams on the vessel.

The oracle's breath caught in his throat. Misfortune came with that sequence. It was a warning. Do not try to cross a dangerous river.

More nervous than hot, he scooped the yarrow stalks

into both hands, allowed the stiff stems to sift through his fingers into the vessel as he slowly considered whether to heed the warning. With his silk sleeve he brushed sweat from his eyes. "I am already in the middle of something very dangerous. I must go forward."

When the oracle called, the artist rose slowly. He had been listening to a song, for in spite of being some distance from the latticed window, he could hear in the garden's solitude the king's youngest concubine sing, *"My gown of silk is cool as jade, my body lotus warm. Come pass the night beneath my willow, wrapped in jade, entwined in flowers."* He sighed. If only he could spend such a night with his fingertips feeling her silk and his chest pressing against hers. It was with great reluctance that he walked into the stifling temple.

"Stand there, by the wall," the oracle instructed. "Prepare yourself." He pulled the cord which shut tight the window slats, darkening the room. In an instant, sunlight flashed through a small hole in one of the slats. On the wall opposite the hole, green willow leaves sparkled, gray roots glowed, the peacock's flared tail glinted fire. All upside down.

The artist gasped. "What is this magic? How have you scattered leaves on the floor, planted roots on the ceiling, made the peacock strut on legs pointed to the heavens?"

The oracle said, "I do nothing. Seven days ago I found a worm crawling along this slat. The creature must have gnawed through the wood and wiggled out. When I closed the slats, the garden came inside with the light from this tiny hole, all upside down."

"Have you seen such images before?"

"None like this. Ghosts come to me when I chew *yiin miao* leaves. This is not from *yiin miao*. Each noon when I close the slats, exactly the same thing happens."

The artist spread his robe wide and looked at the dancing images on it.

"Notice," the oracle said, "the willow which I know is just outside this left corner grows upside down on that opposite right corner. When the peacock perches on the stone bench outside, there, where I know is right, it sits upside down on the left side of the back wall. Reality has not only turned upside down, but left has become right and right has become left."

They stood in the closed room, barely able to breathe. The oracle said, "I cannot explain these images. But somehow you must record them. Perhaps they are a gift from my ancestors." He put his hands on the artist's shoulders, his eyes narrowed. "Listen carefully to me. No one must suspect that such images actually exist."

The oracle opened the slats to dispel the images. Both men stepped outside. But a third man, a spy from the court, remained inside where he had hidden behind the entry screen.

The artist ran through the city's dusty streets to the palace foundry, dodging carts, bumping fish baskets swaying on bamboo poles across the shoulders of merchants. Upside down images swam in his head. How could he record the light show in the dark room? Place an upside down peacock on a plough blade? Craft a wine vessel with leaves at its base?

The foundry perched on the hill along the city's north wall where wind from the south stoked the fires needed to melt metal. Inside the building, other artisans worked.

In order not to call attention to himself, the artist sat on his stool as he usually did and began to make a bronze vessel, although he had no idea what exactly to make. He pinched together a ball of beeswax. By habit, he formed the wax into a small bowl about five inches deep and eight inches across. He stared at it, hoping for an idea.

When another artisan working close by plunged hot tongs into a rain barrel, water hissed and sputtered. The artist jumped.

"What's the matter with you?" the artisan said. "You jump like a cricket."

"That water just gave me a wonderful idea. With this wax, I'll make a water mirror for the concubines of the king. They can gaze into a bowl filled with water and see their beauty reflected." That was what he said he would do. Make a water mirror and give it to the court. Secretly, however, he'd give it to the oracle.

On the outer curve of the wax bowl he carved what he imagined the king's youngest concubine would look like sitting on the bench under the willow. On the willow's thick branch he carved the old peacock, its long, elegant tail almost as beautiful as the woman. Then, directly opposite that scene, across the bowl but on the inside curve, he carved exactly the same thing, but willow, bench, woman, peacock, all were upside down. When the carvings satisfied him, he added script around the inner rim in the custom of bronze vessels in praise of the king whose patronage made the bowl possible.

Then he dipped the wax in liquid clay, let it dry, dipped it again, and once again, until he had a hard clay shell around the wax. After cutting channels in the shell, he fired it in the kiln. As the wax melted inside the shell, it flowed out the channels. Only the hard shell of clay remained. The wax was lost forever.

Lost.

I pause once again to tell you plainly, there was much more to be lost than wax, as I hope you have guessed.

I continue.

After the artist removed the clay shell from the kiln with long tongs while it still glowed with heat, he supported it on a rack. Then from a long handled crucible he poured a blazing stream of bronze into the mold. Bursts of orange, red, and yellow flew from the molten metal and inside the mold the fiery liquid took the shape of a bowl imprinted with the oracle's secret upside down garden as well as the artist's secret vision of the king's youngest concubine.

The full moon rose over the foundry. The south wind blew. The artist sat alone polishing the finished bowl.

With a frightful shout the oracle burst into the foundry and grabbed the bowl out of the artist's hand. "Quickly, we must flee. Now! A spy speaks against me to the king, tells him I harbor evil ghosts. Above all armies, the king fears ghosts. The temple is in flames. My enemy is coming."

"No, I am here." A warrior thrust his sword into the oracle's throat. Blood colored his golden robe red. He fell, the bowl clutched in his arms.

Just one moment later the warrior staggered forward, buckled, and collapsed to the floor with a knife stuck deep in his back. It had been thrust by the strong hand of the palace eunuch. "Go quickly," the eunuch said to the artist.

"You are from the palace?"

"I come for one who cannot come herself. She knows of the magic light, your bowl, and the plot to kill you and the oracle. There is a boat just beyond the north gate where the river turns. Hurry. To the river. Now!"

The artist pried the bowl from the oracle's hand and pressed it tight against his ribs. He scrambled over the wood stacked behind the foundry and ran to the locked north gate. He pushed his toes onto the boards of the gate, climbed up, and leapt down.

Behind him, loud shouts. Between him and the boat, flickering lanterns. Trapped, he had no choice but to plunge into the cold river. Holding the bowl tight in his left arm, he sidestroked slowly to the middle of the river.

"Look. He's there. In the river."

The arrow struck the artist's neck violently. The bowl lurched from his grasp. The current swept away the artist. The bowl tumbled and churned in the moving water, sinking gradually, until it was sucked into the bottom mud and buried.

I'm sure the peacock cried at that very moment. As well it should. I warned you. Nothing good ever comes of secrets or spies.

Yes. The oracle died. The artist died. But the mournful song which the king's youngest concubine sang when she learned of the artist's death flowed over the palace walls, across the river, and into the repertoire of countless sing-song girls in countless wine houses in all of China.

You may ask how I know this. Do not bother. I am a storyteller. I know, just as I also know what I am about to tell you.

The river flowed on, changing course almost as often as succeeding dynasties changed, but the secret bowl remained buried in mud.

Until the thirteenth century.

Then a fisherman snagged it and, thinking it was a carp, happily pulled it up. "Look at this," he yelled. "I've never caught such a thing." Bragging in the tavern that night, in a gesture of bravado, he gave the bowl to the sing-song girl in exchange for extra songs and serious favors.

But the scene on that bowl reminded the sing-song girl of a garden in an old, old song. Frightened, she traded the bowl to a monk in exchange for a lesson on immortality. The monk carried the bowl to his temple high on the Mountain of Flowing Water where he placed it on the altar and filled it with yarrow stalks. The bowl predicted many things.

Until soldiers raided the temple.

They stole the bowl and sold it to a merchant traveling the Silk Road. The merchant sold it to Marco Polo who carried it back to Venice where he presented it to a wealthy Roman whose servant later tossed it, by mistake, into the trash pile behind his villa in Rome.

Listen. Keep up. I am compressing time, glossing rapidly over one event after another. How else will I bring you to the present where this new tale begins?

Just three weeks ago, in our year 2005 CE, a bulldozer excavating a mall site in Rome unearthed the oracle's bowl along with a sorcerer's effigy of a naked lady, a rather plump naked lady, I think, although she was only eight inches tall. Within hours, bowl and naked lady were snatched and smuggled across the sea to California where a wealthy art collector in Monterey purchased the bowl, but not the naked lady. She remains for sale.

The story of the past ends here. Ancient stories are

our beginnings. You must follow the present tale yourself. Leave the shade of this willow. Avoid the soft splashing of the river on those black rocks. And know this. For more than twenty-five hundred years the bronze bowl kept the secret of the upside down garden.

But in California, hardly anything remains a secret.

WEDNESDAY

I

THE NAKED LADY

Sweating in the July heat, Mai Ling elbowed her way through the tourists crammed along San Francisco's Grant Street for Chinatown's Wednesday Market. Cars were banned. Noise was not. People multiplied.

If the handsome Italian sporting the Panama hat and carrying the looted sorcerer's effigy of a naked lady in a football-like brown paper package made better progress than she did, she'd never recover the naked lady for Interpol's Stolen Art Unit.

At a snail's pace, she nudged around booths selling ivory, CDs, silks, and flutes. She bumped against Germans, Japanese, Anglos, dressed in red wrinkled tees, ironed Oxford shirts, sexy halter tops, khaki shorts, Levi's, three inch stilettos, yellow flip-flops, Nikes, all talking, all smelling of sunscreen and ginger blossoms.

Mai, wearing what she considered the perfect disguise, had on a tight black t-shirt, grungy jeans that were threadbare under the back pockets, and dirty tennis shoes. She had spiked her short black hair with gel, made broad swipes with purple eyeliner around her eyes, and silvered her lips with gloss. To complete the Gothic look, she dangled a Celtic cross around her neck, screwed nuts and bolts to her earlobes, and hung a huge black leather purse from its fat strap on her shoulder.

She blended in.

Midway up Grant, the tight crowd watching the University Players perform "The Monkey King" totally blocked the street. The man in the Panama hat plowed his way through but she was stopped dead in her tracks by an animal from the cast. The shabby brown horse unzipped its costume in front of her. The head part neighed and galloped away but the half-man, half-rump stood upright and spoke English.

"Hey, China doll. I bet you'd enjoy a ride on me."

"Not even if you had a whip and wrote for the *Los Angeles Times.*"

Mai pushed the ass out of her way and barged through raucous simians from the cast.

"Actors!" she shouted nastily, stretching her neck to see around pink ribbons on a pony tail and a Forty-niners cap. She barely glimpsed the Panama hat over the top half of the horse as it pranced up, head swaying, bobbing, and flirting. She grabbed its muzzle.

"Look stud. Move out of my way or you're glue." She hooked her foot around his leg and tripped him.

"Bitch," the horse yelled.

"Jerk," Mai screamed.

She looked up. The Panama hat was gone.

Jumping on a vendor's chair, she surveyed both directions.

No hat.

She went into World of Pastry, then up and down the

aisles in Dragon Silks.

No hat.

Into the Bank of Hong Kong. Into Emerald Gifts. Finally down the stairs into Lee's Dim Sum Restaurant. Maybe the Italian wearing the hat went underground, familiar territory for a smuggler.

In the restaurant, a wilted couple and four laughing women stood jammed shoulder to shoulder in the tiny waiting area. Mai scanned the eaters. Good luck. She found him. The man sat at a back table with the Panama hat on the chair beside him. Mai couldn't see the brown wrapping paper, but the brim of the hat stuck up at an awkward angle and could easily be reclining on the plump naked lady.

Sitting opposite the man, in profile to Mai, was a woman Mai knew, Ms. Toni Wilson of Wilson Imports, Ms."at-Wilson-Imports-we-acquire-only-antiquities-with-known-provenance" Wilson. Toni was a billboard for California. At twenty-eight, she looked eighteen. Her straight blonde hair accented sea blue eyes. Her beach tan accented hidden parts. Like a complementary color, she enhanced the dark, handsome Italian sitting across from her.

Toni was a good deal more than a beach babe. She was an artist who worked in bronze as well as a business woman who found good homes for imported art. In fact, just now she was probably negotiating to buy the naked lady. Or facilitating its handover. Or maybe this was just a social lunch, not the final destination of the brown package. Mai would have to keep a sharp eye on everyone.

The hostess behind the cash register asked, "How many?"

Mai answered with a made-up name. "Dawn. Just one."

"Stand to the side. You can look at this menu."

Mai butted up against a fat woman and fanned herself with the menu. She doubted Toni would recognize her in her Gothic outfit but just in case, she used the menu as a shield, peering sideways around it to keep an eye on the back table.

The dim sum cart, stacked high with round wooden bowls of meats, vegetables, and dumplings, moved to the back table. Mai strained to keep track of the dim sum bowls in case the naked lady hitched a ride on the serving cart. But after the cart wheeled on, the Panama hat still lounged on the chair at exactly the same angle.

A table directly in front of Mai emptied and a mad exchange of hungry customers for the full ones occurred noisily as the four laughing women pushed to sit down. At the same time, six Japanese students trudged down the stairs and oozed into the just vacated space. By the time Mai's line of sight to the back table cleared, the Panama hat perched on the Italian's head and he and Toni came towards the register.

Where was the package? It was the size of a football. The Italian's creamy silk shirt was tucked tightly into slim linen pants. He carried nothing. Toni wore practically nothing as if she had molted and new skin took the form of a tan v-neck jersey and beige miniskirt. She definitely had no football size bulges anywhere.

Mai shot a glance at their table. There was no package on the chair. The dim sum cart wheeled away from the table into the kitchen. Two Japanese students waited by the table while a busboy loaded the dirty dishes into a tub, gathered the soiled tablecloth into a bundle, and spread a clean cloth on the table.

Where was the package? It had been on the chair seconds ago. With quick eye movements Mai scanned the room. Everything was as it had been. The only place the package could have gone was into the kitchen, either on the dim sum cart or in the tub of dirty dishes. She didn't dare burst into the kitchen to paw through dishes.

Mai did not anger easily, but this really pissed her off. She'd been bested by some scummy, though handsome, black market trader. A looted artifact passed from seller to buyer under her nose. To cool her rising agitation and get a grip, she fanned herself vigorously with the menu while Toni and the Italian exited.

She'd have to wait here, that's all there was to it. With only one way out of the restaurant, up the stairs, anyone leaving the kitchen with the damn sorcerer's naked lady would have to come this way.

The hostess called "Dawn" and directed Mai to a small table by the swinging door into the kitchen. From it, Mai watched kitchen, cash register, and exit stairway. Because she had a splitting headache, she gave up being subtle and openly gawked in her best Gothic manner, scrutinizing everything that came and went on the dim sum cart. When it wheeled in front of her, she chose a barbequed pork dumpling. Just as she took a bite, a man came out of the kitchen carrying a large laundry bag on which yellow letters spelled CHOO'S. "I'll be right back," he told the hostess and pushed his way to the stairs.

Mai felt like smacking her forehead and shouting, "I am such an idiot." Of course. The busboy scooped up the package when he cleared the table. Wrapped in laundry was how the naked lady would escape. Immediately she stood and threw money on the table. The steaming dim sum cart blocked the aisle.

"Excuse me," she said, and flattened her purse against her chest to maneuver awkwardly around it. By the time she got up the stairs to the street, the man and laundry bag were gone.

And the street was still packed with people.

Mai stopped a young boy and asked in Chinese, "Choo's Laundry. Do you know it?"

"No."

"I do," a younger girl said. "On Washington."

Mai wanted to dash full speed through the crowd but she had to settle for rude walking. On Washington's steep hill, the crowd thinned so she doubled her pace down the sidewalk until she spotted CHOO'S painted on a window on the opposite side of the street. She zipped across.

CHOO's was empty except for one clerk behind the counter. Embroidery across his shirt pocket spelled "Sammy."

"I lost my ticket," Mai lied. "I gotta have my red blouse. Long sleeves, black buttons."

"I need the ticket."

She hoped his name wasn't Sammy Choo. "No you don't," she said. "Mr. Choo never needs it."

"Then next time pick up your blouse from Mr. Choo."

"Right. I'll just look myself."

She pulled up the hinged part of the counter, barged into the back room, and rifled through the clean clothes covered in plastic, coat hanger by coat hanger, but really scanned the area for bags like the one from the restaurant.

"Stop, kid. You'll get it all out of order. Go wait by the counter. I'll look for it."

Mai stomped her foot. "It's a red blouse, long sleeves. I gotta have it."

She retreated to the counter. She felt the blue paper bundles of clean laundry stacked on one end. They were all flat and smooth. No bulges from a hidden package. One by one she picked dirty shirts and trousers out of a canvas bin to the side of the register. She found nothing.

Sammy emerged from the back. "Kid, leave those alone. Go. Come back with a ticket."

She'd seen a drawer under the cash register. She wanted to look in it. "Can't. Party started. I'll call home. Gimme your phone."

Sammy pushed a black dial phone at her.

She stood facing Sammy, dialed a phony number, and backed up against the drawer.

"Mom," she said to an HMO computer voice menu, "look in the desk for my laundry ticket. We can't find my blouse and I need it for the party."

Sammy rolled his eyes. To distract him, Mai waved the receiver and said, "Mom's looking." At the same time she hooked the fingers of her other hand on the drawer and tested to see if it would open. It wouldn't. Probably locked for a good reason.

"Okay. Thanks." She hung up. "My ticket is number 89205."

Sammy turned to look again. Instantly Mai pulled the skull barrette out of her hair and squatted in front of the drawer. In two seconds she had the sharp end of the metal clip in the lock and in two more had the lock picked.

Bingo.

Reclining innocently in the drawer was the brown package. She shoved the barrette into her jeans pocket and reached for the package.

"Hey, whadaya think you're doing? Get out of there."

Sammy grabbed her arm. She jerked free and jabbed her elbow into his stomach. Hooking her other arm around the back of his neck, she slung him over her hip. He thudded loudly when he hit the floor and screamed even louder when she threw the dirty laundry bin on top of him.

She snatched the package and jumped over the heap that was Sammy and smelly linen. Then she sprinted down Washington.

At the curb onto Kearny she stuffed the package into her enormous purse and darted in front of a bus which braked with a hiss. Madly dodging cars, she scooted between an airport shuttle and a limousine and flew up the wide entrance stairs of the very cosmopolitan EastWest Hotel.

In the busy lobby Mai slowed down. A spacious atrium reached upward for two stories. From its high ceiling a mobile of slim aluminum blades turned slowly in the air currents. Midway across the lobby a moving ramp carried visitors diagonally up to the mezzanine.

The whole of the open space mezzanine contained the EastWest Art Gallery. Visitors often came to the hotel just to see the gallery. A kiosk at the hotel's entrance announced that currently twenty Zhou Dynasty bronzes on tour from Shanghai squared off in battle with twenty of Andy Warhol's Pop Art images and Brillo boxes which had traveled from Los Angeles.

Walking casually, Mai followed a French family of five by upholstered chairs and large leafy plants. She cut between *père* and *mère*, sidestepped their luggage trolley, and headed to the piano bar.

No doubt Sammy was careening down Washington hot on her tail. She'd change her clothes and hide out in the bar's Ladies Room.

Whoa. No she wouldn't.

Seated at the bar, her back to Mai, Toni Wilson held a cell phone to her ear. The Italian's hand rested on her arm and his Panama hat tilted at a seductive angle on his head.

Mai veered quickly left. A small tour group gathered in the center of the lobby. The tour leader called, "My group, my group, walking tour of Chinatown, here, here."

Sammy entered the main door holding a cell phone and headed directly toward the bar and Toni. If he noticed Mai in her Gothic outfit, she'd be sprinting again, not walking, through Chinatown. To avoid him, she pushed into the middle of the tour group and shrank lower than the heads around her. From that vantage point she spied a room key envelope sticking out of the back pocket of one gentleman. She acquired it. And kept going. Fast. She squeezed into the elevator as its door was just closing. "*Merci, merci*," she said to the French family, making room for herself by backing two of the children flat against the elevator's side wall. All five gawked at her.

Glancing at the purloined room card for a room number, she punched the button for the eighth floor. The *père* asked her to press twenty-two. The French were going higher.

When the elevator stopped with a slight lurch, she elbowed out. Since the occupant of the room whose key she snitched was downstairs heading for a walking tour of Chinatown, his room should be empty. After she found the room, she quickly swiped the keycard in the door lock and cautiously slipped in.

Caution proved a good thing. From the entry hallway she could see only the ends of two beds. On one, she saw two boy's shoes attached to two socks attached to two legs. A video game blared on the TV.

She shut the door very silently but gasped when her image in a mirrored closet door scared the hell out of her. The feet on the bed gave no sign that she had been noticed. She dodged into a dressing area. Since she could still see her own reflection in the closet mirror, and presumably so could the one on the bed if he looked up from the TV, she ducked into the toilet/shower area and shut that door.

Working fast to change her clothes, she tossed the room key into the tub and emptied her purse. She placed the brown paper package, her money clip, and her cell phone on the back of the toilet. From the bottom of the purse she pulled a blue Valentino sundress, Prada sandals, hairbrush, and a packet of makeup removal tissues and stacked all on the floor.

She turned the empty purse inside out and lifted up two bamboo handles transforming the black purse to tan and began likewise to transform herself. She wiped away purple eyeliner and silver lip gloss, dropped the used tissues into the purse, then brushed madly at her spiked hair until it smoothed out. After she stripped off the nuts and bolts earrings, Celtic cross, black t-shirt, threadbare jeans, and dirty tennis shoes, she jammed them into the purse.

Dressed in sandals and sundress, she reached for the

brown package forgetting the money clip and cell phone on top of it. She caught the money but the phone scooted across the tile floor, clattering and spinning. She grabbed it and listened for a reaction from the room's occupant. All she heard were gun shots and screams. For the first time in her life she was grateful for video games. With the phone and money secured in the pocket of the sundress and the package in the purse, she'd be happy to see herself looking twenty-five again in that closet mirror if she could just get the hell out unnoticed.

She opened the door a crack.

"You get your own Coke," a boy yelled.

"I got yours last night," another yelled back.

Mai shook her head. Why was nothing ever easy? There were at least two boys in the room.

"Come on. I got yours."

"So?"

A newspaper whacked something.

"I'm telling."

"Cry baby."

Mai clenched her teeth. Kids. Someone just get the damn Coke.

"Wait till Mom comes back."

"Shut up. Go yourself if you want a drink and prop the door open so I don't have to let you in again. And bring me one."

Mai watched a boy in khaki shorts prop a book against the entry door and disappear. It took her one second to get out the door behind him.

Walking slowly down the hallway, she kept some distance away from the boy. When he emerged from the ice and snack nook with two sodas, she couldn't resist. She wagged her finger at him and scolded in Chinese as she pantomimed his propping the room door open.

He stared and cocked his head. "Crazy lady," he said.

Mai needed to turn the naked lady over to Interpol right away. She had recovered it. Someone else would return it to Italy. Waiting for the elevator, she typed a text message on her phone to her Interpol contact, "Meet me in Portsmouth."

No doubt Sammy had found Toni in the bar and blabbed about the Goth who swiped the brown paper package. Even though no one here knew that she worked for Interpol, Mai, dressed as herself, didn't want to chance meeting Toni, especially since her bulging purse did nothing to complement the slightly wrinkled Valentino sundress. Toni would look at this purse with great suspicion.

No. She would definitely not go down to the lobby. She'd leave the hotel by the mezzanine exit which would put her on the pedestrian bridge over Kearny.

At the mezzanine Mai stepped out of the elevator and was instantly flattened against its closing door by Toni who came streaking out of the EastWest Art Gallery and collided with her. Her bulging purse thumped against the door. "Good grief, Toni, take it easy," Mai said, shifting the purse to her other shoulder out of Toni's way.

"Mai, I'm so sorry. I didn't see you. It's just that I'm terribly late for an important meeting." The man with the Panama hat, also moving at full speed, caught up with Toni.

Mai flashed a theatrical smile. "Toni, are you sure you aren't running away with this handsome man?"

Toni seemed taken aback. Mai knew very well they both were canvassing the hotel for the Gothic teen after

Sammy's horror story.

Toni recovered in a split second and returned Mai's smile. "Now that would definitely make for a better afternoon. Mai Ling, allow me to introduce one of our new Wilson Imports representatives, Frank Conti."

Frank Conti was the kind of handsome man who actually looked perfect up close. He had the flawless complexion of a Milan model, eyes as intense and searching as a cutting horse working cattle, casually styled black hair, nice nose, full lips. There the perfection stopped. His ethics were fathoms away from perfect.

Mai held out her hand. "Nice to meet you."

"My pleasure." His grip was gentle and he held on to her hand in an intimate gesture. In some other century or on some other planet he might have kissed it. Lord. Mai disengaged her hand and almost wiped it off on her dress.

"I'm in a rush myself," she said, but thought she'd better use the exhibition as a cover for her being in the hotel. "I've a million things to do in Monterey before my own exhibition opens tonight at Coconut Gallery but I wanted to see these bronzes before they are packed off to another gallery."

"I know your show is tonight," Toni said. "That's why I was startled to see you here. I'm coming, of course." Toni's cell phone interrupted. With undisguised exasperation, she said "No" to the caller.

Mai had enough of polite exchanges. She really did have to get to Monterey for the opening of her exhibition of Chinese brush paintings. She stepped aside to let the two into the elevator. "I'll see you tonight, then."

Mai noted the security guard at the pedestrian bridge

exit and two others within the exhibit space, an indication of how very valuable these bronzes were.

"Good morning, Ms. Ling." The gallery manager greeted her with a smile. "I'm glad you took the time to see these treasures."

"I couldn't miss them, Mr. Thomas." Well, she would miss them if she could but now she had to play out the excuse for her being in the hotel.

She walked into the gallery. Standing by one of the cases was Helen Frye, a Ph.D. from Oxford, Chinese scholar and visiting lecturer at the University of California. Mai often ran into her at events, often in Monterey as well as in San Francisco. Helen was a serious supporter of Chinese art.

"Hello, Helen."

"Oh, Mai. You startled me. Shouldn't you be in Monterey?" Her words sped along like the traffic in London. "I've been researching in the library all week and I've come to look again at these Zhou Dynasty bronzes." Still in the fast lane, Helen leaned towards Mai. "You know, of course, about the Chinese bronze bowl in Monterey that Walter Elderson acquired. My research has convinced me it represents a camera obscura." Helen whispered, "A remarkable find. Walter and I have scheduled a news conference for tomorrow."

Mai suppressed her surprise. She knew that Toni Wilson had sold Walter Elderson a Chinese bronze bowl, but that it might depict a camera obscura was news to her. Walter acquired the bowl about the time the naked lady went missing from a site in Rome. A bowl tagged "Number Thirty-seven, bronze, of Chinese origin" was all that appeared on the list of looted artifacts from that site. It must be the same bowl. If it was, a press conference about it would definitely cause a stir, no matter what Helen thought it represented.

"And," Helen continued in high gear, "Louis asked me to mix my Taoist wine for your show tonight."

"Wonderful. Louis and the Coconut Gallery always take good care of me. I'll look forward to the wine and the news conference." Mai thought maybe Helen had already consumed too much of a Taoist concoction. She usually was wrapped very tightly in scholarly propriety, rational reserve, and paisley dresses. As high as she ever got was when she crossed the Golden Gate Bridge. She seemed to be excited about Elderson's bowl, but not drunk.

Mai, however, bordered on screaming agitation. Her Interpol contact waited for her in Portsmouth Square and here she stood, feigning interest in old bronzes.

Along with a few other visitors, Mai peered through the glass cases at the bronzes from 476-221 BCE, China's Warring States Period. She wasn't concentrating well. She had seen these bronzes before in Shanghai and studied photos of them in long hours of memorizing for Interpol.

After what she considered a reasonable amount of time, she had the guard let her out the mezzanine exit onto the pedestrian bridge and dashed over Kearny to Portsmouth Square. A woman in the playground area pushed a baby stroller towards her as she stepped off the last stair.

"Oh, Alice is so cute all in pink," Mai said. She put the purse in the stroller and picked up the baby. She bounced the little girl for a long minute while chatting with the woman. Then she put the baby into the stroller alongside her purse, hugged the woman, made a big deal about getting together for lunch, patted the baby, and left the purse in the stroller. Along with her dirty clothes, shoes, and Gothic jewelry, Interpol had the naked lady.

And Mai still had her raging headache. It showed no signs of abating. Noon had come and gone. She needed to get home. She needed coffee. Her cell phone vibrated in the pocket of her sundress.

2

PORTSMOUTH SQUARE

Mai ignored the cell phone vibrating in her pocket. She walked quickly through Portsmouth Square, a green haven in noisy, crowded, urban Chinatown. She bowed slightly to the card players who knew her and asked about the health of the mother of one. Her cell phone continued vibrating. She ignored it. She had to get a taxi and head home.

But the cell phone insisted. She pulled it out and looked at the caller ID. This she couldn't ignore. She stepped away from the card players into the shade of a tree and answered the phone.

With misgivings, Mai said, "Yes, Grandfather. It's me."

Instead of hello, her grandfather said, "Could you come here right away?"

Mai felt a surge of panic. What on earth was wrong that her grandfather needed her? Was he sick? Had he fallen? A strong sense of guilt rumbled in her stomach. She had let weeks go by without checking in with him. She'd been busy, but not that busy.

She took a deep breath. "Grandfather?" The urgency in her question needed no more words.

"I'm fine, Mai. But I need to talk to you right away. Can you come?"

He sounded his usual healthy self. But if he wanted her to come, something was the matter that he couldn't discuss on the phone.

Appointment book pages scrolled through her head. She was booked solid in Monterey from four this afternoon on. It was now almost one o'clock. If it wasn't an absolute emergency, maybe she could go next week.

A burst of laughter from the card players jarred her thoughts away from her four o'clock appointment. These companions came every day to smoke and sip iced tea and laugh, old friends bound to each other by more than a game.

Mai held the phone without speaking, debating how to respond to her grandfather, distracted further by an old woman who sat alone on the nearby bench unrolling a rumpled paper bag. Mai could feel that paper bag when it was new, crisp. Her grandfather had sent her to school everyday carrying lunch in a new brown paper bag. The old woman's had been reused many times. The thin sandwich she took out fed loneliness more than poverty.

Mai glanced beyond the woman to the playground area where a young father held the waist of his small daughter, a gentle gesture of protection as she climbed steps up the slide.

"Mai? Are we still connected? Mai?"

She heard her grandfather's question.

No, not for a long time had they been connected. She thought it, but didn't say it. She was still searching for words to tell him that she was too busy to come.

Portsmouth Square nagged at her. Card playing friends, old woman, father and daughter. Everyone should stay connected. Thin sandwiches in used paper bags never should be eaten alone.

She hesitated. Which obligations could she cancel?

"Mai?"

"Yes. I'm here."

The little girl climbed the slide again.

Mai found the words. "All right, Grandfather, I'll come."

As often as she had to change directions midstream, she never quite got used to the sudden rearrangement of carefully thought out plans. First she'd have to load her car with clothes for Monterey then drive to her grandfather's summer retreat on the Sacramento River. If she drove fast, she could make it back to Monterey by eight for her exhibition opening.

She caught a cab across the street at the hotel. The stores on Geary blurred as the cab sped west towards the Pacific Ocean and her home in Sutro Heights. She leaned back in the seat. Better cancel Monterey appointments, especially the one with Angelo.

Since Angelo never carried a cell phone and never answered a stationary one, she left a message at Coconut Gallery.

"Louis, let Angelo know something important's come up. I won't be there to do the radio promo with him for his art installation. He'll have to be brilliant on his own. And give my regrets to the Art Guild. I know you'll manage the dinner in solo splendor without me. I should be there for my show by eight."

She flipped the phone shut. Well, she hoped she'd be

there. It was a long drive to Locke. What on earth did her grandfather need?

3

THE CAMERA OBSCURA

Earlier that morning, in Monterey, Angelo woke, rolled to the edge of the futon, and sat up, taking in the energy of the summer crowds outside. He knew it was ten o'clock. The *putaka putaka* of the Harbor Cruise boat's engine was punctual. The voices of tourists below his window waiting in line for the harbor tour of Monterey Bay were distinct.

"Amy, what did you do with the tickets?"

"Where's brother?"

"Stop pushing."

He pressed his feet on the wooden floor of his upstairs, one room studio. As he took several steps to the front window, he rubbed his palms back and forth over his black curls, banishing lingering dreams. He checked out the crowd on the long stretch of Fisherman's Wharf below. Straw hats moved onto the excursion boat, red sweatshirts lined up for ice cream, black camera bags dangled on shoulders. A few boats with white sails skimmed out of the marina. The water gleamed electric blue.

"Perfect," he said. "The light is perfect. It must stay this way all week. I absolutely must have this sun for my installation on Saturday."

At the kitchen sink he filled the tea kettle with water, and when the clicking of the pilot light finally caught enough gas to flame, he set the pot on the burner's medium flame. Leaving the water to heat, he took off his plum blossom kimono, hung it on a closet hook, and stepped into the shower.

With hot water running on his head, he considered making a last addition to Saturday's Coastal Art Illusions installation, one that needed bright sunshine, a risky requirement in this seaside locale. But art, like life, demanded risks.

The tea kettle whistled as he buttoned the silk yellow and orange Versace shirt and pulled on Levi's. He slipped his feet into Gucci loafers.

Sipping instant coffee, he glanced out the corner window at the sun dancing on a hundred masts in the marina and sparkling across the water between him and the municipal pier. Holding the cup in one hand, with the other hand he opened the book lying on his small kitchen table, David Hockney's *Secret Knowledge*. He leafed through several pages, appreciating Caravaggio's use of light. Then he flipped to the simple line drawings of the optical effect of light traveling through a small hole into a dark room creating an upside down and reversed image.

He held the coffee cup frozen midway to his mouth as he imagined his Costal Art Illusions installation as it might be seen upside down in a dark room. It was the same idea that leapt into his brain the first time he saw Walter Elderson's Chinese bowl with its upside down garden scene. The idea clung there fiercely ever since.

What froze the coffee cup midair was one tiny problem. That bowl with the charming upside down garden was supposed to be a secret. Only a few of Elderson's elite friends, including the scholar Helen Frye and the manager of the EastWest Art Gallery in San Francisco, knew of its existence. He was not supposed to.

Okay. So? He didn't have to acknowledge that the bowl generated the idea. He could say he got the idea from Hockney's *Secret Knowledge* and Hockney's thesis that some of the Old Masters utilized such dark room projections to make their paintings. He could say that.

He sipped the coffee. His brain skittered around like the lights off the water in the marina. He could make such a picture show work. It would be extraordinary. He had to risk it.

He left the cup on the table, tucked the large book under his arm, grabbed his baseball hat from the peak of his empty easel, and jogged down the steps.

Angelo's small studio occupied the second floor of a converted warehouse at the end of Fisherman's Wharf that once stored fishing supplies for the tackle shop below. That tackle shop had become the Coconut Gallery, a trendy art space for exhibitions by local *plein-air* artists, or large collages of handmade paper by Taos artists, or sculptures of blown glass by Chihuly.

Angelo had been the first artist to put together a show for the gallery in the days when he painted in oils. One of his paintings still hung on the back wall, a four-by-six foot canvas titled *The Fox*, a portrait of Mai, although few could put the disjointed cubes, dots, and twisted Z's in any anatomical order.

He kept tubes of paint by his easel, but he no longer used them. Instead, he created large installations along California's coast. He had a devoted following, rich donors, and good publicity, especially for this current project, the third in a series he called Coastal Art Illusions. He was covering Monterey's historic Custom House with golden drapery and flying a sculpture of sails above it. And, as of right then, using a camera obscura as a viewing point.

At the bottom of the stairs Angelo smelled the fish and chips frying for early lunch in the Coconut Café adjacent to the Gallery. Gulls no longer roosted on the tops of the pilings but flew in low pursuit of the bait tanks on fishing boats or fought over scraps of bread tossed by the tourists over the wooden railing into the water. Otters played around the rocks close in and farther away seals barked.

He bounced down the rough, tarred surface of the wharf shoulder to shoulder with morning tourists. He passed raw sea creatures displayed outside the seafood market on his left, then crossed to the other side to catch the aroma of clam chowder steaming on the counter at Bernie's, ready to be ladled into paper cups.

"Chowder, Angelo?" Bernie asked.

"Hey, thanks Bernie. Later, for sure."

"How's the project?"

"Great."

A few feet farther, a delivery truck parked in front of the seashell craft store blocked half the walking space. He and two baby strollers dodged around it but he ran into a small hand carrying an ice cream cone and the chocolate just missed his Gucci loafers.

"Oh, little one, I am so sorry," he said, leaning down towards the child. He sidestepped the mess. He pulled money from his back pocket and handed a five dollar bill to the mother. "Please buy her another cone."

He reached Custom House Plaza at the end of the wharf.

"Angelo, over here," the sailmaker yelled from the small space between a large anchor and the railing of the Custom House, clearly the only space to stand without getting pushed about by the crowd.

"The sunlight is amazing," Angelo yelled back.

After Angelo managed to scrunch behind the anchor, the two men shook hands. The sailmaker, tall and thin, was burned a deep brown by years on the sea. His muscular arms would still furl a sail rounding the Horn in a gale, if he ever again crewed a tall ship for the Navy's teaching unit. His blue no-nonsense work shirt made a quiet comment next to Angelo's yellow and orange Versace.

"How can you be so distressingly bubbly, Angelo? Please tell me you have not made another addition to your art event of the century."

"One more, as it happens, but it won't affect you. The drapery design stays as we fixed it. You're quite safe."

"Three days to go. This little 1841 Custom House, in case you didn't notice, is almost sixty paces long and fifteen paces wide, with two story sections on both ends. Takes a lot of fabric to cover it. And I don't have cloth yet. How safe is that? My workers can only make drapes with cloth, not imagination."

Four teenagers walked under the balcony behind them and the sailmaker moved his elbow off the railing. Angelo stepped a little closer to the anchor.

"I talked to London yesterday," Angelo said. "I swear to you the cloth is on a truck in L.A., gorgeous golden cloth. I have a sample bolt in the studio. It will all come tomorrow."

"You'd better hope so."

"You can sew wonders with it."

"I can sew anything." The sailmaker frowned. "But not instantly. To drape this Custom House and get your three jibs flying above it we should have been sewing since June. I'm too old for creative pressure."

Angelo laughed. "You are old, dear friend, but not dead. Wait until you feel this cloth. It falls so beautifully. I promise. Delivery tomorrow."

When Angelo conceived this draping project, it took him a whole year to convince the city of Monterey and the state of California that no harm would come to the old Custom House. By that time he had added a soft sculpture of triangular jib sails to fly above it.

Six months later he acquired the permits for the project. If his previous two environmental art statements had not been written up to critical acclaim in *Western Art Journal* and *New Art Perspectives*, and if he did not have the backing of a very wealthy patron, his ephemeral comment on wealth from the sea lanes would have been dead in the water before one sun had risen and set. His project proposal, including sketches and a lengthy explanation of the whole concept, was bound in hard cover. When that was presented to the city and state fathers, tourist dollars flashed green.

Angelo stepped back into the plaza. His project manager, engineer, and patron made their way though the crowd from the Maritime Museum. He met them halfway.

"Gentlemen," Angelo said to his colleagues, "we'll build a camera obscura right here." He marched off into the plaza.

"A what?" the engineer asked the project manager. Angelo made quick right angle turns, pacing off a square.

"A what?" all three asked in unison when Angelo stopped in front of them.

"A camera obscura," Angelo answered. "It's Latin, 'camera' meaning chamber and 'obscura' meaning dark. A dark chamber."

The trio exchanged glances. The engineer's shoulders slumped, the project manager raised pen to clipboard, and the patron raised his hands in surrender.

"No, no, don't worry. It is magnificent. And not that difficult. We build a simple structure, like a walk-in cargo crate. We make a hole in the side facing the Custom House. Sunlight comes through the hole bringing into the room the image of the draped Custom House." He paused for dramatic effect. "Only the Custom House is upside down and backwards."

"I don't get it," his patron said.

"Simple optics," Angelo said. He flipped open *Secret Knowledge* to the drawing of a tree outside a room and the upside down image of the tree on the wall opposite a tiny hole in the outer wall.

"Look here. Light rays disperse everywhere. Some from the top right of the tree travel in a diagonally straight line through the tiny hole and end at the bottom left of the wall and rays traveling diagonally from the right root end up at the top on the left."

They all stared at the drawing in David Hockney's book.

Without missing a beat, Angelo continued. "A camera obscura is a way to view the golden drapery from a tiny space. Don't you see? The large and the small. It will be magic. Absolute magic! Yes?"

Yes. Yes. Yes. They all nodded without any noticeable trace of doubt.

"Will this be the last addition?" the project manager asked skeptically and handed Angelo the time schedule he had worked out for the construction of the scaffolding for the drapery and the rigging for the jibs.

"I promise," Angelo said. He took the time schedule and studied it. "Yes, this will move us to Saturday with good speed. Just the one additional detail. Hire more carpenters if you need to."

"New job assignments, additional lumber, greater cash flow," the manager said. "I'm afraid we'll need to work this out at the pub over gallons of beer."

"What better reason for beer on a glorious morning," Angelo said, shaking hands with all three. "I trust you completely."

He bounced off towards the wharf, waving a hand as he went, calling "*Ciao*" over his shoulder.

Four steps later he collided with Robert Giles-Smyth, the art critic for Carmel's *Art Wise Press*. With precisely cut gray hair, thin face, pale high cheek bones, and three piece gray suit with a maroon carnation in the lapel, he reminded Angelo of Oscar Wilde's Dorian Gray, an elegant façade for an evil soul. He was distressingly immaculate. Angelo wanted badly to throw clam chowder on his gray trousers or slip dead sardines into the pristine jacket pockets. In short, Bob-The-Critic gave Angelo the willies.

Robert put his hand on Angelo's arm. "I happened to be standing here and heard your wonderful explanation of a camera obscura."

Angelo tried to step around him.

Robert took tiny steps backwards and repositioned himself to face Angelo, rather like a cobra. "Do you think it wise, dear boy, to plan a camera obscura just now. I'm sure you know Walter has a news conference scheduled for tomorrow to announce that his Chinese bronze bowl is a representation of a camera obscura."

Angelo's eyes dared Robert to say more. "Art does not exist to be wise." He leapt around him.

Robert turned and pressed against Angelo's shoulder, keeping pace. "Well, your art certainly does not. People will talk. Coincidence simply does not exist in California. Why expose your, shall we say, intimate connection to Walter and that bowl?"

Angelo tapped the book with a flamboyant gesture, although he felt his jaw tighten. "My project has nothing to do with any bowl. You of all people, Robert, should be familiar with David Hockney's *Secret Knowledge.* I'm simply utilizing a camera obscura to enhance my artistic vision as he suggests other great masters have done in the past."

"You may claim that, but it looks suspicious. Build a camera obscura now and you link yourself to the camera obscura bowl, whether you admit it or not, and thus link yourself to Walter Elderson. Some relationships are personally more dangerous than others."

Angelo outwardly dismissed the innuendo with a head toss, but his fingers tightened around the book and he barged through the line of tourists waiting for chowder at Bernie's. Then he stopped, confronted Robert face on, and threw a dagger of his own. "If you made your own mark in the world, Robert, rather than leeching off other people's creations, you would appreciate risks."

"Walter's funeral, dear boy, socially that is."

"I don't think so."

Angelo did not bounce off. Rather he charged. He hated being pushed into action, especially by a prick like Bob-The-Critic. He wanted to finesse a quiet announcement of his camera obscura as an aside in his promo for the drapery project, not make a big deal about it. He would have to tell Walter what he was up to this afternoon before Bob-The-Critic did in his best weasel fashion.

Angelo followed a group of chattering tourists the rest of the way down the wharf. When he arrived at the Coconut Gallery, the owner, Louis Rosa, bolted out.

"Angelo, thank God you are here. Mai just phoned. She can't be here in time to do the promo with you or the dinner with me. Good Lord. Everything is crazy. I wanted her to decide where to hang each painting. I can't believe it. Her show opens at eight."

Angelo refocused. He handed Louis *Secret Knowledge*. "Take this book and calm down. I'll hang the paintings. She'll be here. Nothing will go wrong."

4

NO TIME FOR BALANCE

Mai paid the cab driver and climbed the steep sidewalk to her home in Sutro Heights. The gulls glided above the Pacific in the warm air of early afternoon. Last night they had sailed on the wind over a sea alive with sparkling, luminescent organisms in a rare light show, a red tide. On her nightly run, along with hundreds of others, Mai had marveled at the shimmering sight. But she only glanced quickly at the sea now.

Pine needles covered the ground around her front yard's gnarled tree, adding the scent of earth to that of the sea. When she pulled open the screen door, the rusted hinges rasped. *Eek. Eek.* She smiled. The usual greeting from the old house.

From behind a wrought iron flower on the screen door she retrieved her house key hidden in a magnetic holder. Inside, she tossed the key on the desk by the door. On her way through the kitchen, she grabbed an apple. Upstairs, she pinned her bangs out of her eyes with tortoise shell barrettes and changed into her blue and gold

UCLA Alum t-shirt and faded jeans, wishing she had time for a run along the beach. She did not. She hurried across the hall to her studio.

Although crunched for time, she still needed to paint a last picture, one for Coconut Gallery's fund raising auction as part of her exhibition. From her window she watched a jay drink from the terracotta birdbath in the garden below. Another jay squawked on a high branch in the pine while a third hopped along the porch railing and tilted its head upward to Mai. She threw the remains of her apple out the window for whichever creature was fast enough to make lunch of it. The birds were a good subject for the painting.

She turned from the window.

Her studio was bare except for a drafting table, a high stool, and her brushes, ink sticks, grinding stones, and rice paper which she kept on a long workbench. Under the workbench, a mahogany cabinet with vertical bins held mats, frames, and glass.

She picked up a length of rice paper and selected three brushes from many on her brush rack. She had no time to sit still for minutes grinding ink, so instead of her favorite ink stick and grinding stone, she grabbed a bottle of ink and a jar of water and carried all to her drafting table.

She sat down on the tall stool.

Thoughts squawked wildly in her head. She couldn't paint at the same time that she puzzled about possible reasons for her grandfather's summons. She suppressed that worry, sinking it to a level of consciousness below the immediate present.

She poured ink into a porcelain dish on the drafting table. In several other dishes she mixed ink with water to make shades of gray. Another feeling interfered. Disappointment. She'd miss doing the radio promo with Angelo. She and Angelo relied on each other in a somewhat strange relationship of mutual caring and regard.

Mai met Angelo five years ago when she was just establishing a reputation in the art circles of San Francisco. A Carmel gallery owner, tired of seascapes, saw her work at a Yerba Buena gallery and commissioned her to do a show of black and white Chinese brush paintings. She called it "Mountains in Winter."

The day "Mountains in Winter" opened in Carmel, Angelo came in to escape Carmel's fog. Or so he said. Her hair was cut in dramatic fashion, short against the nape of her neck but longer at the sides, falling forward along her jaw, with wide stripes of red highlights to frame her face. She had on flowing moss green pants and a loose mauve jacket. A long strand of black pearls fell over the jacket's lapels.

They instantly launched into an easy conversation. When he came back three days later, it was not to escape wet weather but to ask her to pose for him in his new studio on Fisherman's Wharf. So, for the summer, she posed, he painted. He talked, she listened. They traded secrets.

Since that summer, many things had changed. Relationships and crises for both of them came and went along with their respective creative enterprises.

Mai had looked forward to joining Angelo on the radio to promote his Saturday's draping installation. She suppressed her disappointment only to have another negative thought pop up. What was the real reason Toni Wilson and Frank Conti were headed to Monterey? Toni seldom attended Mai's exhibitions and Frank probably needed to feel dirt from a dig site on a piece of art to make it worth his while.

Mai breathed slowly, six counts in, six counts out. Curiosity, disappointment, and worry receded.

At last, aware only of the need to paint, she smoothed the rice paper gently on the felt covering the drafting table. She listened to the jays squawk, visualized their bright bodies, the sharp angles of their claws, the energy in the quickness of their hops, the individual feathers of their wings.

In one continuous, powerful stroke, black ink became the crooked pine branch. Shades of gray became feathers spread in flight, and open beaks, and angular claws.

When she finished, she wrote with a small brush down the right lower side the Chinese characters for "Three Hungry Birds painted by Mai Ling." She pressed her signature seal first in red cinnabar paste and then into the paper under the black calligraphy.

The birds' eyes seemed to dart. Their claws pushed off the rough branch with power. And they squawked. The painting had enormous energy.

"Uh-oh," she said as she stood to look again. There was no element of serenity to offset the energy, no yin to balance the yang. Her grandfather would notice that. "Perhaps a quiet bird on the ground," he might say. Angelo would notice and probably say, "The painting makes me nervous."

It was too late to fix it. She couldn't just add another bird. It would throw the composition off. There was no time to do another picture. Balance was out of the question. So was the time consuming final process of mounting the picture on heavier rice paper.

She rinsed the brushes in the corner sink and pulled out a mat and thin ebony frame with glass from the vertical bins under the workbench. She'd put the jays in that western style frame when she got to Monterey. For now, she wrapped heavy paper loosely around picture and framing parts.

Downstairs, she put the picture in her leather portfolio. With the portfolio clutched under one arm, she grabbed her suitcase with one hand and with the other picked up her garment bag full of silk dresses for a week of gallery signings, lectures, and television interviews. When she pushed the screen door open with her foot, the hinges cautioned, *Eek. Eek.*

Damn. She plopped everything down in the doorway and retrieved the key from the desk where she'd tossed it.

Anything else? Did she forget anything besides the key?

Yes. Her lucky charm.

Upstairs, she took her necklace out of the dresser drawer and slipped it over her head. She always wore it to her shows, a small peacock on a silver chain, a present from her mother on her fifth birthday. Although she could no longer remember the sound of her mother's voice from that long ago birthday, she remembered her blessing. *You are beautiful, like the peacock. May your life be full of beauty always.*

Running down the stairs, she tucked the peacock charm under her t-shirt. Outside, she moved the luggage out of the way, locked the door, and hid the key behind the screen's wrought iron flower. After laying the portfolio on the passenger's seat of her Jaguar, she angled the suitcase into the convertible's small trunk and flattened the garment bag across it.

It was about a hundred miles to Sacramento, then another twenty-five south to Locke. Hoping traffic wouldn't be as bad as the crowds at Wednesday Market, she put the Jaguar's top down and her sunglasses on. She squealed her tires out of the driveway and sped off in her blue car under blue skies. Automatically she checked her rear view mirror out of habit to see if anyone was following her.

5

FLOWERS FOR ALL OCCASIONS

At one o'clock, about the same time that Mai's Jaguar sped towards Locke, Cypress de la Mer, in Carmel, opened her flower shop. She usually stayed home on Wednesdays, but she had four special orders to fill.

Cypress was born too late for 1967's Summer of Love, but she clung to its legacy as if she were its only flower child, innocent, freckled, and rustic.

Cypress owned Carmel Floral Treasures and re-created flower power in a number of ways. She specialized in "roadside" arrangements most often composed of sunflowers or birds-of-paradise accented with twigs, thistles, mustard blossoms, or an occasional orchid stalk. Her creations were in great demand on the peninsula, and a weedy arrangement of hers in a hotel lobby, art gallery, or private dinner party was considered *très chic*.

But she had a secret. In and out of Carmel Floral Treasures, along with flowers, a stream of antiquities flowed, objects that had been carried across Europe on Crusader horses, across Asia on Silk Road camels, over oceans on Dutch, English, and Portuguese trade ships. They were soldiers' spoils of war, travelers' souvenirs, commerce. They'd been dug up, taken, sold, for centuries. Or yesterday. Like all such objects in museums, private homes, or auction houses, some came with known provenance, the property of an established collector or museum. Some, like all such objects in museums, private homes, or auction houses, had no traceable history of ownership. Of these, Cypress said simply, "they came from an anonymous collector in Switzerland." The floral arrangements generated cash, the ancient treasures, wealth.

In truth, both aspects of Carmel Floral Treasures provided Cypress with a solid purpose in life while deep unhappiness chipped away at her soul.

To open for business, Cypress hauled terracotta strawberry pots and small birdbaths out to the sidewalk under the shop's front window. She hung a wreath of fresh daisies intertwined in pine boughs on the door and she straightened out the lengths of Indian brass bells hanging on the inside doorknob.

After checking the thermometer in the refrigerated case to the right of the counter, she went through the glass beads hanging in rainbow sequence, red-orange-yellow-green-blue-indigo-violet, from the archway between the front and back of the store and brought from the workroom little white daisies, bold yellow sunflowers, delicate purple iris, and arrogant orange birds-of-paradise. She clumped them in white plastic tubs on the floor around the room. One tub of daisies she put outside next to the door.

When all was arranged, she pulled a match from a wooden cylinder on the counter, lit a long incense stick, and watched its drifting smoke fill the shop with the lemony scent of sweet flag, *acorus calamus*, or, to Walt Whitman, leaves of grass. He wrote his Calamus poems under its glorious influence. Cypress liked Walt Whitman.

In spite of the Food and Drug Administration's prohibition against consumption of her favorite plant, Cypress enjoyed more than the scent of sweet flag. Throughout the day she drank tea made from its leaves or nibbled on jellied candy made with pectin, sugar, and boiled roots. Occasionally she wove herself a garland of its aromatic leaves and topped her natural brown curls with it. Sweet flag, she argued, mainly to herself, produced heightened creativity for her and Walt Whitman. She liked Walt Whitman.

This afternoon she had four orders to fill. In the back workroom she finished the last of the four by sticking just one bird-of-paradise into twigs in her own handmade pot. One by one she brought the bouquets out of the workroom and put them on the end of the counter to the far right, out of the way, for her delivery driver to pick up.

She pulled open a drawer and got out four delivery tags and a calligraphy pen and was inking in the first tag when she glanced out the front window and saw flaming red hair, a bright Hawaiian shirt, black leather pants, and cowboy boots on a guy astride a candy apple red Harley.

"Hunter!" she said, a bit too loud. "Why does he always materialize at the worst possible moment?" Irritation screwed up her handwriting.

She watched Hunter maneuver his Harley to the center of the parking space in front of her shop, exactly parallel to the curb. After he kicked the kickstand down and swung his leg over the seat, he walked to the tub of daisies under the window. He pulled out several and shook the water off them before rattling the doorknob several times to jangle the bells. He made a dramatic entrance.

Cypress cursed to herself. Out loud, she said, "Aloha, Hunter," as if they had last seen each other at breakfast instead of more than a year ago. Careful not to betray any hostility, she continued. "What brings you so far from Rome to our little hamlet?"

"Your happy, smiling face," he said and presented the daisies to her.

She stuck them behind her right ear and curtsied, mocking the gesture. "And people say you are not a gentleman."

He took the pen from her hand, put it on the counter, and lifted both her hands out to her side. "Let me look at you. Signature flowers embroidered on that fetching peasant blouse and madras skirt over very enticing hips." He leaned over the counter. "Ankle bracelet and cute beaded moccasins. Why, Cypress, you don't look one day older than sixteen."

"And you don't look one day wiser."

"*Touché*," Hunter said and burst into a rolling laugh. He let go of her hands and walked to the refrigerated case, examined several stalks of lavender *bletilla striata*, selected one, and carried it to the counter.

"Orchids? My goodness," Cypress said. "Who's your lady this trip?"

"I'm here for Mai's show. Put this in with a few iris and several blades of sweet flag and send them off to Coconut Gallery."

"Mai will be so delighted," she said, in high pitched

exaggeration.

"You're full of snappy responses today." He spun in a complete circle as if examining the room. "I see sarcasm still lingers about, never having left the shop."

"We could only wish that you had." She jabbed her pen at him.

"*Touché*, again." He hit his hand on his chest and jumped back in mock pain.

She ate a jellied candy from the dish by the cash register and offered him one. Before he could take it, the bells on the door rang and Robert Giles-Smyth, in his art critic's gray suit with maroon carnation, entered, looking a bit wilted.

"Cypress, good afternoon. I am in need of a grand display for a spur of the moment dinner party tonight."

Hunter moved to the baker's rack of pots along the side wall so Robert could stand at the counter.

"Robert, hello," Cypress said. "I know exactly what you want." She walked to the tub of sunflowers. "Let me arrange some of these with a few marvelous black twigs. I'll fix it up in a bronze glazed vase."

"Oh, you are a lifesaver, Cypress. That sounds divine. You know my address. Please deliver C.O.D. and thanks ever so." He let the door slam shut behind him.

"'Flounced,' is the appropriate word, I believe, for that gait," Hunter said, coming back to the counter.

Cypress shrugged and wrote out an order form. "He's an art critic. He always walks like that. Imparts a sense of importance."

She continued writing and changed the subject. "So, you are here for Mai's show. Chinese brush paintings can't be hot items in your antique shop on the Via Giulia."

"Nope. Not at all," he said. He walked behind the counter and popped two sweet flag candies in his mouth. "Actually, I picked up a couple of items in Rome to sell to Walter Elderson." He slipped his arm around her waist.

"Picked up something for him or plan to pick up something from him when he isn't home?" She pulled away.

"I see that along with your incredible sarcasm, your powers of ESP haven't dimmed."

He held up the pot with the bird-of-paradise. "Did you make this pot? I remember a potter's wheel in the back."

"Yes, as a matter of fact I did."

He slowly turned the arrangement, looking all around the pot. "Both pot and glaze are excellent. You could make a living selling just these."

"I do."

"Liar."

She wrote out a tag for the pot in elaborate calligraphy. He straightened the daisies in her hair, pushing them off her cheek. Cypress sensed the protective leather tips come off their fencing foils.

"There's a lot of buzz on the street about a certain Chinese bronze bowl in town. Tell me about it, Cypress." He leaned towards her.

She leaned away. "My knowledge here in Carmel is limited. We are not as cosmopolitan as Rome. The Via Giulia knows more than our Ocean Avenue."

His flat hand hit the counter hard. "Damn it, Cypress. You do know. Tell me how Walter Elderson got that Chinese bronze bowl. It should have been mine. I watched that mall site in Rome for months for excavated relics."

It was Cypress's turn to burst into a delighted laugh. She couldn't help it. Hunter played a rough game and the image of him skulking about a shopping mall excavation site was priceless. "Now, that is a rare picture." She moved around the counter and patted his cheek.

He hit the counter again, not so hard, then began his tirade again. "The very day those first artifacts surfaced, the antiquities chaps had that site secured. We have laws against looting. Who the hell got that Chinese bowl off the site?"

Cypress needed her strength to draw blood in a different battle for that same bowl later in the day. She didn't want to waste energy on Hunter. While picking a handful of iris from the white plastic tub, she calculated what information was safe to pass on. "Word here on our little turf is Wilson Imports. New guy. Good looking. Frank Conti. He was in Rome watching the site with sharper eyes than yours, apparently."

"That's not funny, Cypress."

She pushed the iris into his chest, dripping water on his leafy shirt. He took them. She grabbed the orchid stalk off the counter and went through the beaded curtain to the back workroom.

He followed. "Wilson Imports? Is that how Elderson got it? There's more to the story. Tell, Cypress. I'll buy you dinner."

Cypress filled a replica Ming vase with water from the workroom sink. She picked up scissors and snipped the stems of the iris to different lengths, pushing her luck with silence.

Hunter tapped the counter with a discarded stem. "Come on, Cypress, you know more."

"Word on the street is that Wilson Imports sold it to Elderson fast to get it off market. I'm afraid your quest for that artifact is yesterday's news."

"Maybe." He put his hand over the mouth of the Ming as she was about to insert an iris. "Elderson didn't have a million plus to pay out, did he?"

Her own quest was not yesterday's news. She had a buyer for that bowl and a plan to get it. She would only tell Hunter what she thought he already knew. She lifted his hand off the vase and put the iris into it. "That bronze bowl wasn't worth a million plus until Dr. Helen Frye got a look at it. Until then it was just another old Chinese bowl."

Hunter took a hundred dollar bill out of his wallet and laid it by the Ming.

Cypress picked it up. "That'll cover the flowers but there's an additional delivery charge, you know. Coconut Gallery is not within walking distance." She wanted the tip of her fencing foil against his heart, the blade bowed.

He kissed her cheek. "Don't forget to add the sweet flag. I have to see a man about a bowl."

"What about my dinner?"

"I'm good for it," he shouted, halfway to the door. "Tonight. Cannery Row. Wear white. For purity."

Cypress thrust the foil into his heart. Last summer she'd almost slept with him. She wasn't about to rerun that sitcom. "If I'm not there, fill your plate without me," she yelled after him.

The Indian bells rattled as the door closed.

When the bells quieted, she set a pan filled with water on the hotplate. With her flower scissors she cut a blade of sweet flag into half-inch segments, dropping them into the water for tea.

"That bowl isn't yours yet, Hunter," she said, stirring the steeping mixture with the point of the scissors.

6

SCOUTING

Hunter sat on his bike at the curb in front of Carmel Floral Treasures, delighted to have wrested information from Cypress's archive of back alley knowledge.

On the Via Giulia he had a shop full of antiques of known and unknown provenance. He didn't really need a hot bowl. Not that all his artifacts were above suspicion. But Rome was his turf.

If Cypress was right, the bowl's journey from Rome to Monterey began in the hands of a novice working for Wilson Imports. That news hit him hard. A novice. How was that possible? He was a pro and some new guy beat him?

Pride. Where would he be without it? He had to get the bowl as a matter of honor. And rumors were flying in the back alleys that the bowl was worth megabucks. No question. He had to get it.

And get it fast. He suspected that, given enough time, Cypress would get her floral prints all over that Chinese bowl.

Or Mai Ling.

In fact, Mai Ling was his real competition. He had tangled with her before. Two years ago she made off with his Alexandrian scroll before he even suspected her pretty face. Now he knew better. She was Interpol. Sly like a fox.

But it wasn't really competition he minded. It was losing. More precisely, losing to a female. He knew damn well that Mai Ling wasn't just hanging around innocently presenting an exhibition of her paintings in a town where there was a freshly looted artifact. This bowl was more than a challenge. It was a chance to even the score.

So Elderson had it. But where exactly did he have it?

Hunter pulled his cell phone out of the Harley's saddlebag and dialed.

"Dr. Elderson, Hunter here. Just got in town. I have the two jade Buddhas we talked about. Certainly, and the letter of authenticity, definitely fifteenth century, Ming Dynasty. Very well protected in bubble wrap. Now a good time to bring them around? Good."

He motored up the hill out of Carmel onto Highway 1, through downtown Monterey, and into Pacific Grove. He remembered that Elderson's Pacific Grove mansion was a classically inspired Greek villa approximation rather than a Spanish Colonial like most of Monterey, and it was about a mile from Cannery Row across the street from the bay. Half of the house was hidden from the street by a tall eugenia hedge. That was all he recalled. Although he'd sold Elderson a few paintings last year, he'd not been inside the mansion.

He needed to know the layout of rooms.

He steered the Harley slowly past the mansion, made a U-turn, and came back to the driveway entrance but did not turn in. He stopped, balanced the bike with his foot on the curb, and studied the half circle of lawn which bordered a semicircular driveway and the mansion.

The mansion was a two story, white structure with four Doric columns supporting the roof and framing an entry porch recessed behind them. A second story balcony above the porch likewise hid behind the four columns. Possibly, in the dead of night, he could slip inside through the balcony door if he could climb a column like a monkey on a tree. Which he couldn't.

A large picture window at ground level to the left of the porch would be easy to get in if it had not been a solid pane of glass. On the second story, two windows matched the height and width of the picture window below but there was no way to get to them on the flat face of the house.

He pushed off from the curb, turned right, and drove up the side street which was one of the mansion's boundaries. Another tall eugenia hedge completely obscured this side of the yard except at the gap for a short driveway to a detached garage.

He turned right again at the next street, the back boundary. The hedge continued but ended at a service access driveway into the yard, probably a gardener entrance. The hedge began again down the third side of the lot along an alley. A neighbor's hedge, equally tall, made the alley into a tunnel.

He'd have to walk the grounds to find entry points.

He drove back to Elderson's semicircular driveway, turned in, and took a bundle of bubble wrap from the saddlebag. As he walked up the path lined with roses to the front porch, he discovered, to his right, a patio garden in the process of being landscaped and a small pond. The garden was hidden from the front street by the hedge and had a glass door entrance into the house. Good.

A cry startled him. A bird of some kind. Or a baby. In the hedge. A baby yelling in the hedge? He puzzled about it for maybe a second. Whatever it was, it clearly screamed, "Help. Help."

Without really caring what was crying, he climbed the three stairs of white marble and walked between two columns onto the shady porch. He studied the lock on the carved wooden door, a tricky lock to pick. Two narrow windows flanked the door.

He scooted around one of two large white urns overflowing with red geraniums that stood in front of the windows and peered inside. He could just make out a fancy foyer with twin staircases curving up on either side and, on the wall to the right of the door, a security system keypad. Bad.

Okay then. He'd just get inside and find out if the Eldersons were going to Mai's exhibition at Coconut Gallery and leaving this nice Greek approximation empty.

Let the games begin.

He rang the bell.

7

GHOSTS

Mai drove the winding River Road, Highway 160, past rows of pear trees and staked grapes, the irrigated orchards and vineyards where years ago Chinese immigrants like her grandfather's family worked the levee farms along the Sacramento River.

The town of Locke was built on just nine acres of the Sacramento delta in 1915 by Chinese workers. Then it was a crowded, booming place. Now it was a dilapidated relic, designated a National Historic Landmark in 1990. Mai knew she would find ghosts here, a handful of residents, a few summer tourists, and her grandfather.

She turned the Jaguar off River Road and down a short hill into a gravel area where she parked in the shade of a pear tree.

To look for her grandfather, she walked up the gravel drive to Main Street and stepped onto the walkway that went the length of the street under rickety balconies supported by old posts set either in bricks or buckets of cement. On the short, narrow street, one building was a small grocery, one a gift shop. Most were empty.

She stepped over a dusty black dog sleeping against a cement tub in front of Al the Wop's, the only bar and restaurant in town. Four touring bicycles rested in the street outside Al's and a few yards down the walkway, three tourists came out of the old gambling house preserved as the Dai Loy Museum.

Mai poked her head into Al's. The mangy stuffed ostrich still stood in the corner as it probably had since the dawn of fermented beverages or at least as long as she had been coming here. The four bicycle riders, wearing UC Davis t-shirts, sat at the bar discussing traveling the Sacramento on a side-wheel steamboat.

She saw a familiar face. She greeted her grandfather's neighbor who sat at a table eating spaghetti, steak, and bread, Al's standard meal. She was a fulltime resident of Locke and taught school in Sacramento. "Good afternoon, Mrs. Nelson. Have you seen my grandfather this afternoon?"

"Mai, how nice to see you. Yes, Dr. Sung and I talked this morning in the garden."

"Your melons are growing well?"

"Very well."

"My grandfather will be jealous. Thanks. I'll find him in the garden."

She continued along the walkway and then turned left into a narrow wooden plank passage between the unsafe, rickety buildings which barely maintained a vertical alignment. At the end she stepped out on the only other street in town, Key Street. Here were the old residential buildings, one church, and four small houses with porches and narrow front doors framed by two little windows.

Mai walked to the one with ceramic pots overflowing with fragrant honeysuckle on the tiny porch. When she stepped up onto the porch, insecure boards moved slightly downward under her foot, creaking.

Inside, she smelled oil paint. To her left, by the narrow window, a painting sat on an easel. It was of mottled green and yellow trees, a wide river, and a figure pushing a small boat into the water. Her grandfather must have just finished it, the paint still glistened and brushes were drying in a Mason jar on the window sill.

This tiny front room was her grandfather's haven, a quiet space far from his hectic medical office in San Francisco. Instead of carefully designed ergonomic office furniture, here was one floral print soft chair, there one floor lamp, and over there a narrow table along the wall which served as a writing desk.

She read a few sentences on the yellow legal pad on the desk beside the *New England Journal of Medicine*, something about new cardiology techniques. She looked at the four books on the shelf above the desk just to see who was keeping her grandfather company this summer. She thumbed through Andrew Robinson, *The Man Who Deciphered Linear B* and Yasunari Kawabata, *The Master of Go*. She read several poems in Daniel Bryant, *Lyric Poets of the Southern T'ang* before replacing it next to the tattered copy of the *I Ching*.

She went into the bedroom. A single bed was covered with her grandmother's blue and white quilt. That quilt was as familiar to her as breathing, although her grandmother had died before she had been born. On the bedside table was a black and white photo she had seen many, many times, her grandmother holding an infant. Each time she looked at the photo, she tried to see that infant becoming Lily, her mother. But she couldn't.

Water pipes banged in the kitchen.

"Grandfather, I'm here," she said, walking to the kitchen.

"Hello, Mai. Thank you for coming. Let me wash this melon."

The kitchen was big enough for the sink and stove but not for the apartment size refrigerator which sat outside on the little back porch.

When he turned to greet her, she noticed his face seemed fatter than usual, maybe because of the round, wire frame glasses, but his body, under a loose tan shirt, was trim and fit as always, except for a hint as he turned of the same tension she felt.

"I hope your melons measure up to Mrs. Nelson's."

"Actually, hers are better. Walk out to the garden. I need to finish watering."

They walked along rows of fragrant onions and garlic. The scents reminded her of sizzling oil and popping garlic cloves and late night dinners he cooked in their San Francisco home when she was growing up.

Her grandfather uncoiled a long hose, settled the nozzle in a row of melons, and then turned the spigot, flooding the row. She knelt and pulled weeds along a stretch of onions, anxious to hear the reason he had sent for her but knowing better than to ask.

When she had a small pile of uprooted weeds, her grandfather scooped them up and dropped them beside the spigot. After tightening the spigot, he coiled the hose, meticulously arranging each loop.

"You have weeded and I have watered. The garden is

fine for today. We can eat."

In the kitchen he cut the melon in half, removed the seeds, and handed her a spoon. They stood at the sink, scooping bites of melon. The house was stifling. The sun moved westward. Time pushed her towards Monterey and Coconut Gallery. Still, she had to wait patiently, respectfully, for her grandfather to choose the time to explain. She pressed her lips together as she had learned to do as a child to avoid blurting out her thoughts.

"Let me put the rinds in the trash," she finally said. When she came back from the porch, she could wait no longer. She asked, calmly, politely, "Grandfather, why did you send for me?"

"Let's sit down."

They moved to the stuffy living room. Her grandfather sat down at the desk. Mai walked to the easel.

"You are painting again, Grandfather. I'm glad. Is this a picture of a fisherman on the Sacramento or the Yangzi river?"

"Both."

"And the brushes are clean and dry. It is finished. Locke is a good place for you to spend the summer."

He put the *New England Journal of Medicine* on top of the yellow legal pad and the pencil on top of that as if he'd completed whatever he was working on. He walked to the easel, took a brush from the Mason jar, and rubbed the bristles against his palm. "I can paint here but not in the city. I planned to stay through August, but something has occurred."

He pulled the desk chair around to the floral print chair. "Please sit down in the soft chair, Mai."

She sat. She waited. Finally, her grandfather, sitting

close to her, said, "Listen to me, Mai. There is an obligation from the past, a duty bound to male heirs."

She heard "duty." She heard "male heirs." Her spine stiffened, the words rang like steel against her. She tried not to voice the hardness she felt towards the notion that destiny without sons was tragic. "I think I can understand that kind of duty."

"I know you can." He took her hand in a gesture she knew from childhood. It was a warm, comforting hand. In it she felt no hesitation, only trust. "I am never disappointed in you," he said.

She relaxed a little and returned his gentle grip.

He spoke in a quiet voice. "Let me explain. Long ago, a monk in a mountain temple in China had a bowl. The bowl came to him from a tavern girl, a singer of folk songs in the thirteenth century. She sang a long song for the monk. It told of a garden with a willow tree, a peacock perched in it, and a woman sitting on a bench. Time and war turned the garden upside down. The monk held the bowl which the sing-song girl handed him. On it were two scenes, a right side up garden on the outer curve, an upside down garden on the opposite inner curve. He said, 'The eye sees one way, the heart another. But each knows change.'"

Mai's grandfather sat silent for a minute. He swallowed hard before continuing. "The monk kept the bowl and gave the task of caring for it to our ancestor, a boy of ten. For two years the boy carefully replaced the divining yarrow stalks and polished the bowl with a sacred cloth so that no dust would obscure its wisdom, for the monk told him that the bowl held a great truth. But misfortune came. Soldiers looted the temple. The boy ran. From behind a tree in the woods he watched while everything of value was taken, including the life of the monk. Our ancestor, ashamed that he had run away, vowed to fulfill his obligations to the bowl by returning it to the temple. He searched for it all his life. Just before he died he instructed his son to look always for the bowl, rescue it, and return it to the temple. And so the obligation passed from generation to generation and eventually came to my father."

The room sweltered in the afternoon sun. Mai felt drops of sweat on her nose. Her grandfather wiped his face with a handkerchief and leaned back against the wooden slats of the chair. He spoke again. "I never believed that such a bowl existed."

Mai watched him intently. He had told her many stories, never this one. He had many burdens, the lives and deaths of his patients, the death of his wife which left him to raise their three year old daughter, Lily, by himself. Then, twenty years ago, when Lily and Mai's father were killed in an auto accident, he became the only family Mai knew. He was mother, father, and grandfather. She remembered how often he looked worried. Never did she dream his burdens went back in time, century before century, to a boy hiding from a slaughter and a bowl recognized from a song.

At first she was puzzled. Why had he told the story to her now? What was the urgency? Her thoughts raced as she tried to make sense of it. She twisted in the chair. Finally she made a connection. The conversation she'd had with Helen Frye in the EastWest Art Gallery echoed in her head.

She spoke softly. "Do you believe Walter Elderson's Chinese bronze bowl in Monterey is the bowl that was lost in the temple slaughter?"

"It is as my father described it."

She tilted her head. Old legends. Dusty beliefs. "That seems impossible, Grandfather."

He stood by the desk and straightened the pencil on the medical journal. "I agree." He looked into her eyes and smiled his usual smile. Then, even more slowly, he said, "But, Mai, do you see a way I can ignore the possibility?"

"You are to return a bowl to a temple? Where is the temple?"

"I do not know. My father called it only the temple on the Mountain of Flowing Water."

She shook her head. "A difficult task."

He nodded as he sat down again, close to her. "Will you steal it for me?"

Oh my God. So that was it, the reason he called me. To steal a Chinese bronze bowl from Walter Elderson.

Her job at Interpol was to recover looted artifacts. The operative word was "recover." She took treasures off the street to return them to their country of origin before they lost a cultural connection in a private collection.

Her grandfather's request to rob a private home struck her like nothing else she could imagine. She didn't like the feeling.

Her silence must have seemed like a refusal. Her grandfather took her hand and pulled her from the chair. "It is too much to ask, Mai. I apologize."

"No. No. I was thinking."

They stepped out onto Key Street for a cool breeze. The street was no cooler.

"Mai, I am sorry," her grandfather said. "I acted without considering all the ramifications. I have been overwhelmed since James Chang told me about the bowl the other day when he came for lunch at Al's. Maybe he can work something else out."

Her uncertainty flared into an anger which she couldn't contain. "You told James Chang about your obligation to the bowl before you told me?" She couldn't believe it. An ancient family secret, and he told James Chang when he should have told her and nobody else.

"James is my oldest friend," her grandfather said. "We went to school together here in Locke. I told him of the song, the bowl, and the temple when we were ten. That is why he came to me about Walter Elderson's bowl."

"But your oldest friend is my Interpol boss. I'm feeling odd," she said. "It's a bit awkward, don't you think? A theft ring made up of you, me, and my Interpol boss. James Chang is an attorney. He should have more scruples than I about delivering a Chinese national artifact into private hands."

She very nearly stomped her foot the way she did as a child, but instead she walked away from him, all the way down Key Street and across the levee to the river. A great blue heron flew off the water. The green river slowly sparkled by.

Why did she do that? Get mad at him. When she was a child, he'd help her with a school project. The phone would ring. An emergency at the hospital. Instead of feeling grateful for the help he had time to give, she'd feel slighted and jealous. The way she felt now.

She took a deep breath.

She wasn't a child any longer. Her grandfather's life extended beyond hers.

"Mai?" He had walked to the levee to get her.

"I'm all right. I'm sorry. I'm glad you asked for my help. Your obligation to the past is worth all I can give you. Let's continue your destiny."

Back inside the tiny house, she stopped by his painting on the easel. "This is a picture of the Sacramento River and the Yangzi? Your personal waterways?"

"Yes."

She felt a quick, momentary sense of danger. "There are many snags in both rivers."

"I do know that. It is not without a great deal of thought that I ask you to do this. You are skilled in ways I am not."

She turned to face him. "I am your granddaughter. My obligation is to you. At any cost, I will steal the bowl for you."

Mai's grandfather wrapped his arm around her shoulder and hugged her. "I love you," he said solemnly.

"And I love you."

"We are good to go?" he asked.

Mai smiled, pleased that the tension between them was gone and amused by his uncharacteristic slang.

He walked to the shelf above the desk and pulled down the *I Ching*. "Let's do one more thing. We have no yarrow stalks. We'll use coins to consult the oracle. Let's see how we stand now and if good fortune will be in the future." He took coins from his pocket.

Mai never consulted the stories in the *I Ching* to predict the future, except with her grandfather. Old legends. Dusty beliefs. She stood so she could see the coins fall on the desk. He sorted out three pennies.

"Is your memory still good?" he asked.

"Since I was nine I could name the trigrams."

Even without practice, she could remember the meanings in the coin tosses. Three heads equaled old yang, two heads equaled young yang, three tails equaled old yin, two tails equaled young yin.

Her grandfather tossed the coins for line one of a trigram. Yin. Again he tossed. Line two, yang. Then line three, old yang.

"What is the name of this trigram?" he asked.

"Wind."

Three more tosses, old yin, yin, yang. "Mountain," she said. The hexagram was Mountain Over Wind, Number 18, Work, in the *I Ching.*

"Mountain Over Wind will tell us our present situation," he said. "Are you ready?" He turned the pages in the book of changes, stopped abruptly, and looked up at her.

"What?" she asked.

"I have never had the oracle give a more appropriate answer," he said.

Mai leaned over his shoulder and read. She was hard pressed to explain the coincidence. "Wow." The six lines extolled the virtue of following a father's work. "That is so right it's scary."

"I agree. Delightful, though," her grandfather said. "Now we have to make a second hexagram with the changing lines to get a prediction for the future."

In her head Mai constructed a second hexagram, changing old yang to yin, old yin to yang. The changed hexagram was Fire Over Water, Number 64, Unfulfillment.

"Uh-oh," she said.

Her grandfather, too, knew the text, turned the pages to the end of the book, and interpreted. "Not a good time to cross a river. A fox got its tail wet trying. We should not proceed rashly. We may be in the middle of a river, but we are not across."

"We can heed the warning. Proceed no further," Mai said, in deference to the oracle's warning.

He looked sternly at her as he did when she was a child.

Mai could tell he was upset by the prediction, for deep down he felt a certain truth in the *I Ching*. But she never shared that belief in fate as predicted by the old stories. She wanted to move him out of this serious concern. So she bowed, as she always had as a child. "We can step into the water and try not to get our tails wet in either the Sacramento or Yangzi."

He startled at her humor. Then he smiled, his shoulders relaxed, and somewhat hesitantly he returned the coins to his pocket. Then he put the *I Ching* back on the shelf.

"Good. I'll pack a few things in a suitcase. I want to go to Monterey with you. I can stay with James in his Pebble Beach house and be out of your way. Besides, it will be good to visit with him."

"Are you sure?"

"Yes. This is a deep river. I want to be near you in case anything happens."

Something always happens. She didn't say it. Instead, she said, "Everything will be fine. Let's hurry. It's four-thirty."

She removed her portfolio from the passenger seat and barely got it and her grandfather's small suitcase jammed into the trunk. She put the top up. She drove the Jaguar onto River Road, a bit too fast.

"Take it easy, Mai. We need to travel two hundred

miles with no damage."

She nodded, preoccupied. She didn't believe in oracles. Still, after the *I Ching's* selection had been so right about their present situation, she found it hard to ignore its warning about their future. She felt a tiny bug of foreboding crawl across her chest, its tiny feet padding out "this may be a river of no return."

8

ENCOUNTER WITH A HARPY

It was late afternoon when, with a jangle of Indian brass bells, Cypress closed the shop. She tagged Hunter's arrangement of iris, sweet flag, and the stalk of orchids "To Coconut Gallery," and left it on the counter for her delivery driver to pick up at six. She snuffed out the incense on the counter and went back through the beaded curtain.

In the workroom she took off her long madras skirt and put on khaki gardening pants, replaced the embroidered peasant blouse with a drab work shirt, and slipped out of her moccasins and into Doc Martens, tying the laces tight. She was ready to tackle her next project, Dr. Walter Elderson and his Chinese bronze bowl.

Walter Elderson, rich, elegant, tall, with stylishly graying hair, was a plastic surgeon who fancied himself both a medical creator of beauty and a primo collector of beauty, with public and very private collections from each category. Beautiful lovers, beautiful art. Possessions.

Cypress counted herself lucky that she was not his type. She had, however, sold him a few pieces of gold both Aztec and Egyptian. And he had commissioned her to landscape his new garden and koi pond in a semi-Asian manner now that he was interested, this year, in Chinese culture and relics. It would take her some time to select the five, ten, and fifteen gallon pots of hyacinths, lilies, and sweet flag for Elderson's garden and load them in her van.

In the Hilton's salon the barber whisked several trimmed hairs from Walter Elderson's monogrammed shirt collar before he splashed a few drops of Calvin Klein's Escape into the palm of his hand and patted Elderson's neck.

"That should do it for another week, Doc."

"Thanks, Henry," Walter said, easing out of the barber chair. He paid the receptionist a hundred dollars, tipped the valet twenty, and drove home.

He parked the Mercedes on his side of the double garage, exited by the garage's rear door, and strolled through the camellia and rhododendron shrubs that complemented the veranda which stretched along the back wall of the house. He stepped onto the veranda, disengaged the house alarm with his key remote, and entered the dining room.

He called, "Edna, are you home?" Hearing no answer from his wife, he began whistling. Things had been particularly strained between him and Edna lately, more so than in any of their thirty years of marriage. Previously, after each affair, he managed to inch his way back into her tolerance, if not her good graces. Things weren't going so well this time and he did not want another strident lecture on propriety.

Upstairs he changed into his running suit, put his bottle of nitroglycerine in the pocket, and looked at his watch. He could go for fifteen minutes one way and then turn around. Half an hour was all he could manage without getting dangerously winded. He left the house by the front door and jogged across the circular driveway to the street.

The early evening fog was still distant on the horizon. He could run down and back before he got too damp. He jogged along the coastal path next to rocks and water at a pace half his former speed with twice the effort. But he had a body and an ego that needed to stay fit so he pushed himself to maintain a routine. He did not want to look fifty any more than his plastic surgery patients did.

When he completed the round trip, he felt a slight twinge in his chest but he circled his shoulders forwards and backwards and twisted his torso for several minutes before crossing to the house. Walking up the circular driveway, he glanced toward the side garden.

What was Cypress doing here this time of day?

Cypress had three pots of sweet flag webbed together for easy carrying in her right hand and a ten gallon iris in the other. The Elderson's groundskeeper knelt by the koi pond spacing several pots. A peacock, which Walter had purchased for ambiance in his new garden, strutted just ahead of Cypress. "Put the lilies and hyacinth directly in the water, George," she instructed.

Walter intervened. "No, don't. Let's wait until tomorrow."

Cypress countered, placing the trio of sweet flag at the edge of the pond. "Oh, Walter, you have no soul. At least let's get the sweet flag in the ground with this heavenly evening light."

"No. George can do it tomorrow. Take off, George." He wanted Cypress gone before Edna came home. Any woman alone at the house with him, desirable or not, would evoke a tirade from his wife. And he was on shaky ground with Edna at the moment, very shaky ground.

George pushed the wheelbarrow to the tool shed.

Walter walked on the flagstone path towards the house. Cypress caught up with him at the glass door into the library.

"We need to talk, Walter. Privately and seriously."

Past experience told him that Cypress would not leave until she prattled on about whatever she had come for, so he held the glass door open for her and noted that she steadied herself on the door frame for a brief second. They walked through the library, turned left down the hall to the nearest of the twin staircases which spiraled upward on either side of the foyer. Cypress climbed with her hand on the railing.

"You smell like a citrus grove, Cypress. Must you always burn and ingest that plant? You are outside and inside sweet flag. Why don't you try gin or something civilized if you want to get drunk?"

"*Acorus calamus*, dear Walter. If Walt Whitman wrote impressive poetry under its influence, you really should try it. Maybe you could come up with an advertising jingle for your practice or, at the very least, an ode to facelifts."

They were at the top of the stairs. Walter glared at her. Cypress, apparently not intimidated, said, "Besides, it's been planted for centuries to keep away evil fox spirits."

"Clearly, Cypress, that part isn't working for you."

He continued down the hallway to the first room on

the left, his private art gallery. He punched in a code on the security lock, crossed the room to the light switch on the opposite wall, and tapped the head of a marble harpy to disengage the alarm connected to the light.

Walter had invited Cypress into his chamber gallery on several occasions when he wanted to show off a new piece or get her opinion on its value. But she hadn't been invited recently. He rested his hand on the head of the marble harpy which stood on a small pedestal to the right of a glass case, its dark bird wings spread menacingly and its woman's face wickedly watching. Cypress rolled her eyes. "Walter dear, we have gorgeous Greek goddesses for sale, you know."

"Gin?" he asked, opening the tall double doors hiding the bar.

"If that's your best offer." She shrugged, surveying the entire room. "The harpy is quite interesting, Walter, but this is much better" she said, moving behind the leather chair in the center of the room and stroking the life-sized metal Medusa, a dozen silver snakes writhing on her head, her golden wings enclosing the space above the leather chair, and her bronze hands clenching the chair's back, ready to pull it over.

As Walter poured gin, then tonic, into two tall glasses of ice, he said, "I placed my two favorite statues so that the harpy perpetually torments Medusa whose metal eyes have no power to turn the harpy's already marble figure to stone."

"How very like you."

"I thought so. My analyst loves that I have them, grist for a lifetime in his psychobabble mill. He thinks it's significant that I chose them since I rake in baskets of money transforming ordinary women into perfect beauties." He dropped a quartered lime in each glass.

"Maybe they remind you of someone? No picture of Mother anywhere," she noted, obviously siding with the analyst.

"Nor of you either, dear," he said, handing her the gin and tonic which she lifted in a toast. Then she backed up and sank down in the leather chair under Medusa, sipping slowly.

"Now, Cypress, talk fast. What's this all about? Why are you here?" Walter said, moving closer to the harpy.

"Well," she answered, leaning into the leather and crossing right leg over left, "I know all about your cute Chinese bronze bowl there in the case."

"That is hardly a unique claim." Walter was standing with the harpy's head level with his, so that both its eyes and his looked directly at Cypress.

"Ah. A privileged few do indeed know about it," Cypress said. "But I happen to know it recently was covered in dirt in Rome. You see, I have friends, Walter. Good friends. Antiquity dealers, bankers." She finished the gin and tonic and lifted the glass for more. "I have a particularly good friend who is an auditor."

Walter took the glass, refilled it, and handed it back to her. She settled into the chair, cozy under the wings of Medusa. She sipped deliberately, slowly. "Your own auditor, it seems, is rather concerned about obvious sums of money coming into your accounts from Wilson Imports. He wonders if you are taking in laundry for that deliciously blonde Toni Wilson."

"You are drunk."

"I don't think so. But I could get drunk one day and

talk to the wrong someone, Edna maybe."

Walter stopped swirling his drink.

Cypress continued. "Edna's such a saint. She tolerates so much from you. God knows why. I wonder what her limit is. She might have more than her usual cause for concern over your relationship with a woman if she knew you were cleaning money in exchange for artifacts." She handed him the empty glass. "Your closet seems to be full of many skeletons."

The clock in the hallway chimed six.

"Go home, Cypress."

"No. I'm quite serious. I'm here to trade that nice little Chinese bronze bowl for silence."

"If you aren't out of here in two seconds, you may suffer a permanent silence."

"Walter, Walter. Is that any way for a physician to talk? I want that bowl. I'll just wait here for Edna. I know she was at the hair salon at four. I expect she should be arriving momentarily."

Walter put both glasses down on the bar. "You know I can't let Edna find a female up here, even you." He put his hand on the glass case but did not open it, options flying through his head. He had no intention of letting Cypress walk away with the bowl. But Edna's impending arrival was a formidable obstacle to negotiating with her. He decided the most immediate way to get Cypress out of the house was to give her the bowl. Then he'd make a call, get a certain friend to pressure Cypress into silence and take the bowl back before the night was over. He did have contacts.

Cypress remained in the chair like a ticking time bomb. Finally, she said, "And one word of caution on a separate matter. Hurt your current lover in any way and it will cost you a hell of a lot more than one little bowl."

He turned to face her. "Since when do you have a heart?"

"Since you don't."

The harpy and Medusa exchanged killer stares.

"Look, Cypress. You have the advantage, for the moment. Do not even think of selling the bowl to anyone in this town. Remember, I know more than a few things about you."

"Of course, dear Walter. We can trust each other on this." She pushed herself out of the soft chair and moved unsteadily to the case. "That's it? Between the two jade Buddhas?"

Walter slid the case open and carefully removed the bowl. Cypress grabbed it immediately in both hands.

"Take it easy, Cypress. It's not a cheap imitation or one of your phony garden statues."

"Beautiful blue-green patina," she said. She turned it around, looked for seconds at the images on it. "So, this upside down garden scene is what all the fuss is about? Imagine."

"Just get out before Edna shows up."

Cypress walked down the stairs clutching the bowl with one hand, the stair rail with the other. Wobbling a little, she went into the library and out the glass door onto the flagstone walkway. Directly behind her, Walter watched with a surgeon's eye for a possible way to remove bowl from hand.

Cypress moved with an unsteady gait. Before she could swerve around the koi pond, her foot caught on the plastic webbing linking the three sweet flag plants. Shaking her foot to free it, she hopped to keep her balance.

Walter seized the opportunity. He rushed at her from behind and pushed with both hands, launching the bowl from her grip. It arced into the pond.

"Damn you, Walter." She swirled around and smacked his chin with a straight arm backhand. He twisted her arm and rammed it into her shoulder joint. Her knees buckled, but she grabbed his legs and held on, her face plastered against his knee.

"Damn you, Cypress." His knee smashed her nose.

Blood spurted. She let go. Her head cracked against the flagstone.

A sharp pain stabbed Walter's left chest and shoulder. He clutched his chest with one hand and fumbled in his pocket for his pills with the other. He pressed a nitroglycerine tablet under his tongue. While sucking on it, he slithered into the water to get the artifact. Squatting in the waist-deep water, he trolled with both hands for the bowl.

The peacock strutted over.

After several seconds, Walter felt the edge of something hard and pulled the bowl up and placed it on the rim of the pond.

The peacock pecked it, sounding three quick tones. Walter put both his hands on the flagstone to hoist himself out of the water. The peacock pecked the backs of his hands. "Get away." He shoved the bird.

Sitting on the pond's rim, breathing heavily, he looked at Cypress laying stone still, her nose no longer bleeding. In the soft evening light, she looked dead. Another sharp pain shot up his left chest. A dead body was not an outcome he anticipated. Now what? No time for major undertakings.

He made a split second decision to leave the body there and get quickly back inside before Edna arrived. She wouldn't see the body. She never came out to the garden. No one driving by would see it either. It was hidden from the street by the eugenia hedge. It would just have to stay there until he could get back to it later that night.

He could not trail pond water into the house. Edna would notice that. So he stripped off shoes, socks, and running suit, rolled bowl, shoes, and clothes together, pressed as much water as he could out of the bundle, and ran naked to the house. After streaking through the library, he dashed to his right down the hallway to the kitchen and into the laundry room. He lifted the lid on the washing machine and, after extricating the bowl from the wad, jammed in running suit and shoes.

He heard the garage door rattle.

Edna. She always punched the automatic door opener as she waited to cross the traffic on Ocean View Boulevard. He grabbed a dish towel and wrapped it around the bowl as he ran down the hall, up the stairs, and into the gallery. He replaced the bowl in the case, threw the towel on the bar, picked up both gin glasses, and turned off the light which would automatically reset the security alarm when the door closed. He flew out the open door and collided with Angelo.

"What in hell are you doing here?" Walter said with a strident voice.

"What in heaven are you doing naked with two glasses in your hand?" Angelo asked, raising one eyebrow. He descended step by step with Walter. "Why does it smell like sweet flag in here and why is Cypress's van in the back?"

Walter pushed the two glasses into Angelo's back and hustled him past the library into the kitchen. "Look, Angelo, I'll explain tomorrow. Please, it's very important that you get out of here. Now."

"I have to tell you about the camera obscura I added to my installation."

"Are you crazy? Edna just opened the garage door. Scram."

Walter knew Angelo had entered by the kitchen door as he often had and could escape out the side gate into the alley eugenia tunnel where he would have parked his Jeep.

Fighting to stay calm in the face of calamity, Walter put the two glasses in a kitchen cupboard. He would wash them and get rid of the body after Mai's show at Coconut Gallery. He sped down the hallway but his bare feet slipped on the waxed hardwood floor and he landed flat, sprawled ungraciously at the library door. His heart beat rapidly, his pulse drummed loudly in his ears, and his chest hurt. But his nitroglycerin was in the washing machine in the pocket of the running suit.

He heard Edna's high heels on the kitchen floor. He pulled himself together, managed to stand, and sprinted up the stairs into the bedroom's master bath, stepped into the shower and turned the hot water on full force. Steam filled the room.

Edna poked her head in the bathroom door.

"Why is Cypress de la Mer's van here? Is she planting? Don't use all the hot water. And hurry up."

He put his hands on the shower wall and leaned forward. This was like a major screw-up during surgery. He'd have to stay calm. Keep his hands steady. Fix it somehow.

As soon as he got back from Coconut Gallery, he'd deal not only with a body and a van but with blood on the flagstone.

9

IN THE DRAWING ROOM

On the narrow River Road Mai couldn't push the Jaguar too fast. On the freeway, though, she raced.

"Mai, caution," her grandfather said, more than a few times until she settled down at a steady speed.

She needed to figure out a way to steal the bowl. Her picture of Three Gorges hung in the Eldersons' dining room but she'd never been in their home so she didn't know what obstacles a thief might encounter.

And there was Angelo. He was involved with Walter. How the hell could she steal a bowl from Walter Elderson without Angelo knowing? Or, a sudden chill ran through her, how could she steal it without Angelo's help? Gallery openings were stressful enough without cold premonitions whirling in her head.

Angelo. She remembered his broadcast. "Do you mind if I listen to the radio? I think Angelo's promo for his draping installation should be on about now."

"I'd like to hear it. He could promote a horse's tail

and make us think it was high art. Still, I'm a little dubious that he'll actually get that Custom House covered in fabric."

"He will." She smiled and scanned the frequencies for Bob-The-Critic's radio program, "In the Drawing Room."

When she found the station, Mai adjusted the radio's volume a little loud to hear above the wind whistling by.

On the radio, Bob said, "Good evening, California. Welcome. It's seven o'clock and this is art radio and I am your host, Robert Giles-Smyth. We are in the drawing room tonight with Monterey artist Angelo. So glad you had time to stop in, Angelo." His voice was compromised by occasional swings into a dry cough.

"Thank you, Robert. Always a pleasure to discuss my work."

Mai moved into the slow lane to pay closer attention. She hoped Angelo would ignore all of Bob's snide comments. "Just redirect the enemy's energy," she counseled him more than once. Her grandfather adjusted the seat to a slight incline.

Bob launched into the interview. "Well, Angelo, we are looking forward to this weekend when you are presenting a site specific installation in Monterey, I believe."

"Yes. This is actually my third production along the coast. My best, really."

"Our audience will remember," Bob said, "that it was two years ago Angelo made that haunting, and I might add, rather eerie, fishing net sculpture in San Diego's Little Italy. Correct? And last year it was the electric light bulb lighthouse off Pigeon Point. I saw that from the sea. Very, very remarkable."

"Thank you, Robert. Both worked astonishingly well. Environmental installations are rather dicey. I loved the good reviews, yours included. Always glad to uplift the critics as well as the audience."

"Let's hope we are all uplifted again on Saturday," Bob said. "Tell us about this new piece."

"For this installation, I am enclosing Monterey's historic 1841 Custom House in a golden wrap of drapery. It will be breathtaking."

"And its meaning?"

"I think," Angelo said slowly, "golden nylon is just totally indicative of commerce and symbolizes rich opportunities from the sea. A powerful comment on Monterey's historic dependence on the sea."

"You mean sardine fisheries?"

"No. No. A hundred years before that. Monterey was the major port of entry on the California coast until the 1849 gold rush when San Francisco's wealth attracted big clipper ships with huge cargos to sell and our little port languished. Until then, though, our Custom House meant money from the sea."

"So on Saturday we will see the Custom House as a golden opportunity."

"Robert, darling, that is exactly why you write your column and why we all read it. You are sometimes very right."

"I'll take that as a compliment, although I must say sometimes your compliments are, if I can borrow your own words, rather dicey. Like your art, I'd say. Haven't I heard that you've added a second installation to complement the draping? Something called a camera obscura?"

Mai almost lost control of the car. "Did he just say what I think he said?" One hand tightened on the steering wheel, the other turned the radio's volume way up.

Angelo said, "Right you are Robert. I've added a camera obscura viewing station. I want everyone to see the installation in both its reality and in a magical way."

"This is new to the project?"

"Quite new. I added it this morning in a moment of inspiration."

Robert cleared his throat. "Did your early morning muse fly low over Fisherman's Wharf?"

"And drop something seagull-like? Robert, you are never obtuse. But you know, as strange as that may seem, that is sometimes the way art works."

"So a passing gull told you about a camera obscura and to our delight we will see one on Saturday."

"Absolutely. I know in our audience tonight there are many who have seen the old camera obscura behind the Cliff House restaurant in San Francisco. Big yellow walk-in box labeled Giant Camera. It falls in and out of repair, is open or closed since the 1950s."

"I do know that structure," Robert said. "Uses lenses and mirrors, I thought, to project the surrounding ocean into the little dark room. Not exactly art."

Mai heard Robert cough again to clear his throat and Angelo cough as if to control his pitch. Her own throat was dry.

Angelo kept talking with a detectable irritation in his voice. "Art is where you find it, Robert, darling. My camera obscura uses no lenses. It is absolutely without technology."

"Just how old is the camera obscura optical effect?"

"Very old indeed. As far back as Aristotle," Angelo said.

"Greek?" Robert paused. "Maybe even Chinese, Zhou Dynasty, around 500 BCE?"

Mai's dry throat sucked in air, her teeth clenched. The Jaguar rumbled onto the weedy shoulder of the road. Her grandfather grabbed the steering wheel and angled the car back into the lane. He shot a look of dismay at her.

"Sorry," she said. "I'm a little surprised by Robert's question."

Angelo plowed on, sounding in control of the interview. "Well, Robert, China is possibly the first country to record camera obscura images. That is a recent speculation based on a Chinese bronze bowl in the collection of our friend, Walter Elderson."

Mai's elbows straightened and her foot jerked on the gas pedal. "What the hell is he doing?" She never talked like that in front of her grandfather. Her face went bright red.

"Watch that semi, Mai." Her grandfather changed his seat to its upright position.

Robert said, "Angelo, the phone lines are blinking. We want to know more about your muse and your camera obscura. You are close to Walter? You've seen the bowl?"

"Darling, I have seen everything that is important in this town. As for muses, they like to keep secrets. What is most important is that each person in the audience comes on Saturday, sees my draped Custom House, steps inside my camera obscura. I promise each of you will be blown away."

Mai was definitely blown away. Taken aback. Baffled. She punched the radio off. "Why? Why? Why did he do that? He never told me anything about adding a camera obscura."

"Why does he do anything? Because he can't contain an idea that has its claws around his throat," her grandfather said.

"Well, he threw off that monster idea at a really bad time. It wouldn't be hard to steal an obscure bowl that the public knew nothing about. After that promo, everyone will be curious. Bye-bye obscurity. Everyone will be dying to see that bowl and it will be more than a little obvious when it goes missing. Lights. Camera. Action. We might as well film me carrying it off."

"I think we hit our first river snag," her grandfather said, worry evident in his hesitant tone.

Mai knew that tone. She regretted venting her agitation, causing that tone, but her head was spinning. She needed time to figure out a plan, a week, at least. But, more than that, she wanted everything to seem easy, keep at least the appearance of cool competence in front of her grandfather.

"No. Not a snag. Pebble maybe." She shrugged her shoulder in an effort to toss off the anxiety. Then she smiled, a little calmer. "First I have a serious talk with Angelo about his big mouth and then I get the bowl."

She raced through Monterey and Pacific Grove. After giving James Chang's address to the security guard at the entrance of 17-Mile Drive, she sped faster than was safe around the curves of the darkening road, the sea on the right crashing against the rocky coast, spray glistening in her headlights.

Turning into the hills above Pebble Beach, she shifted the car into second, shifting her thoughts to the clock on the dashboard. Everyone, press included, waited for her at Coconut Gallery.

"I didn't think to bring clothes for your opening," her grandfather said.

"That's okay." She really hadn't expected him to come. Although he usually saw all her paintings before she exhibited them, he'd been in Locke and she'd been traveling. "You and James can come anytime on the weekend. I'll meet you there and give you a special tour."

At James Chang's gate she punched in the security code and drove through just as the gate opened wide enough for the car to squeeze by. She accelerated down the long driveway to the villa.

"Easy, Mai. Go patiently and carefully. With everything."

"I will." She braked incautiously to a halt at the bottom of the driveway, jumped out, and pried her grandfather's suitcase from the trunk. Before he could pick it up from the flower bed where it landed, she was inside the car again, hollering out the window, accelerating up the hill. "I'll call as soon as I can. Don't worry. I'll figure something out." Although, she continued the sentence to herself, probably it won't involve either patience or caution.

10

COCONUT GALLERY

Mai lugged her suitcase, garment bag, and portfolio with the painting of the squawking jays into her room at Casa Munras Hotel in Monterey. After a two minute shower, she styled her long bangs so they almost hid her eyes, dressed in silk, and drove the short distance to Coconut Gallery, telling herself to concentrate on the immediate present and nothing else. The bowl was a future problem.

In spite of the Lot Full sign in front of the marina, she pulled in, waited for a bakery truck to pull out of a yellow loading space, and then parked the Jaguar in it. Even before she got out of the car, she smelled fish and seaweed.

It was eight-thirty. Both Custom House Plaza and the wharf were crowded with well-dressed tourists. At the end of the wharf, tiki torches flickered in front of the Coconut Gallery. The gallery owner, Louis, fired them up on special occasions.

She tried sprinting down the wharf, but her high heels caught in the uneven tar covering the old boards, so she slowed down and paid attention to where she placed her shoes. Midway down the wharf, an animated fiberglass clown in front of the ice cream store serenaded her heartily. "Ho. Ho. Ho."

"I love sea level," she said jokingly to a stranger.

When she reached the tiki torches, she looked behind her out of habit, checking the faces before she pushed open the double doors of the Coconut Gallery.

Instantly she relaxed.

The gallery was full of warmth, vivid colors, and the fragrances of perfumes, flower arrangements, and Taoist cinnamon wine. Louis, playing host, greeted her wearing a very expensive white Italian suit with an extra large silver handkerchief spilling out of the left breast pocket.

"Mai, the show is magnificent. Your birds are singing and your plum blossoms bring joy to winter." He kissed her hand.

"Thank you, Louis. Sorry I'm a bit late." She scanned the walls, locating her koi, stallions, the waterfall tumbling from a craggy cliff, bamboo in the wind, a boat among lotus. She patted his arm. "Your presentation of the pictures is excellent."

"All Angelo's doing, of course. Now, Mai, do enjoy the wine and the guests." She would. She loved this role of successful artist.

Directly in her path was a floral arrangement in a replica of a Ming vase on a pedestal, two purple iris and one orchid stalk dwarfed by tall lemony leaves of sweet flag.

Uh-oh. *Yiin miao*, the drunken plant, foxbane.

Cypress wouldn't waste the drunken part on an arrangement for Mai and there was only one person who would send foxbane. Hunter. It was his spicy calling card, a reference to her Interpol name, The Fox. He and Angelo both knew that name. Angelo didn't deal with Cypress. This was Hunter's floral taunt as a competitor. It said, "I'm here. I'm planning to steal an antiquity."

Cripes. The Chinese bowl. He was after the Chinese bowl. Her pulse momentarily shot sky high.

But she had no time to dwell on possibilities.

The regular first night crowd of artists and admirers quickly surrounded her. The serious ones in black cotton were artists. The smiling ones in splashes of color were admirers. And off to the side was a sullen one in gray summer wool, the art critic.

If she painted humans, she'd paint this crowd, each portrait a person of importance, witty, intelligent. Each a "someone."

But Mai felt like the best someone of all.

She wore a lime green Chinese silk dress covered in hand embroidered pink roses with dark green leaves and blue butterflies with golden tipped wings, silk stockings, and high heeled cherry silk shoes. Jade earrings peeked from behind her short classically cut hair which smelled of jasmine. Her peacock necklace sparkled at her throat.

Mai stood in front of her painting of a rooster at sunrise. Its flamboyant tail feathers and elegant long neck spoke volumes. She answered a young artist whose hair smelled of turpentine. "No. No. Actually, I do admire male strutting."

Three women joined Mai and the young artist, their scents overriding Mai's jasmine, but not the turpentine—Chanel No. 5, St. Laurent's Opium, Armani's Georgio.

"This one," Mai said of the next painting, "is my favorite. The cranes swooped over the snowy bridge on a very cold afternoon. The brush strokes are quick. I wanted to capture the wind."

The young artist, holding his wine glass close to his lips with cobalt blue smudged finger tips, waved a hand at the pictures and asked in whispered confidence, "Do you actually believe the world is so simplistic that it can be depicted in black and gray?"

She was not surprised by the question. She'd heard it often from other artists who painted with color. But she admired the Chinese style which considered black a color. Without elaborating on that, she said, "The world is as we see it. Only its meaning do we invent. If cobalt blue serves your meaning, it is right for you. Those cranes, for instance. You see them as simplistic. Others see them as symbols of longevity. To me, they are moments. I paint moments. For me, ink captures time."

"Can I quote that?" the gray critic asked, standing close by with pencil and pad in hand. He had no scent of his own.

Mai grinned broadly. "Certainly, Robert. Always glad to help you fill the page."

Robert Giles-Smyth, standing with Edna Elderson, put his notepad and pencil in his pocket. "Mai, you know Edna."

"Yes, I do. Hello, Edna. I'm so glad you and Walter could make it tonight."

"Edna is the only person I know who can look absolutely ravishing in a Chanel suit," Robert said.

Well, maybe not ravishing, Mai thought. But certainly elegant. Edna's ash blond hair swept softly back to the nape of her neck in loose curls. Her beige, boxy jacket was trimmed in red, and even with pleats, the black skirt fell slim and smooth on her hips.

Two other artists came up to engage Mai in conversation. She adjusted her position so she could also pay attention to Robert and Edna. "Warhol's tomato soup cans, notwithstanding," was the last she heard from one of the artists before she tuned him out and listened instead to Robert.

"Anything new in your closet, Edna?" Robert asked.

Edna did not lower her voice. "You mean other than the current rotation of lovers?"

"Ah, yes, sorry about the latest. Why don't you just divorce and be done with it?"

"And lose these fascinating social outings?" She drained her wine glass and picked up another off a waiter's passing tray without missing a beat. "I suppose you also know about that stupid peacock." She snarled ever so slightly. "With Walter, this year it's all things Chinese, last year Egyptian, next probably Estonian."

Robert said, "A peacock is rather appropriate, don't you think? Walter can probably teach it a thing or two about strutting and preening."

Toni Wilson cruised over. She was ravishing. She wore black jersey which clung to her tan surfer form. "Everything is beautiful, Mai," she said. She nodded a familiar "hello" to Edna and touched Robert's arm. "Can I have Robert for a second? I want to introduce him to our new representative, Frank Conti."

"Gladly," Edna replied. "I'll get more wine."

Frank Conti lounged in a far corner. Mai didn't want to talk to him. Edna probably didn't want Toni anywhere near Walter. Mai followed Edna to the bar. At the bar Walter Elderson sipped from a large glass of cinnamon wine. He handed another glass to Edna.

"Dr. Elderson, nice of you to come," Mai said and extended her hand. She noticed red scratches on the back of his hand when he shook hers. Uncharacteristic blemishes.

"My pleasure," Walter said. "Edna and I love the lotus. Just the thing for an empty spot in our foyer."

"Wonderful. Louis will take care of it for you." She leaned towards the bar. "Helen, your wine smells wonderful. I enjoyed the bronze exhibition this morning in San Francisco."

"I've been studying each bronze there," Helen said, "for clues about Walter's. They were of no help. But I'm so excited. I found in the university's archives the text of a book discovered in 1969 in a third century BCE tomb dug into a hill above the Liuyang River. It was written on bamboo strips bound with hemp. It's a record of Zhou Dynasty magic."

Helen filled a blender with ice, red wine, and a dark cinnamon concoction, the ancient Taoist recipe part. She must not have heard "In the Drawing Room" because she looked a bit smug, if agitated, in muted pink, her brown hair pulled back in a severe bun. Art to her was a historic puzzle, not beauty.

Walter raised his voice over the whirling blender. "Helen and the manager of the EastWest Art Gallery in San Francisco are showing a remarkable interest in my new acquisition," Walter said to Mai.

Helen turned off the blender and came from behind the bar. "For years I've studied everything related to the Zhou Dynasty. When I saw Walter's bowl, something clicked in my head. A reference to a bronze bowl feared by a Zhou king. Two days ago I finally found the reference. That tomb book from the Liuyang hill records magic illusions produced by court entertainers." She stammered. "Think of it. In 200 BCE a book discusses upside down images in dark rooms. And," she gulped some wine, "refers to a lost bowl. Walter's bowl has to be that bowl. Its value to history is enormous. Please, Mai. You must help me convince Walter to lend it officially to the university for study."

Walter winked at Mai. "Spoken like a true, but bankrupt, scholar," he said. "Not a chance, Helen. A Zhou wine jar sold in auction at Christie's for nine million."

Mai said, "I understand that your bowl has a woman on it. That alone is very unusual for 500 BCE. And an upside down scene. I have never seen a real artifact from that date with either."

Walter put his empty glass on the bar. "Christie's rep is coming to appraise it tomorrow. Maybe she has." His tone was friendly but his dismissal of Mai's scope of experience was not.

The reference to her limited knowledge zipped over Mai's head. She was happy to keep facts learned in her role with Interpol a secret. But she almost choked over the Christie's rep business. River Snag Two. If Walter was going to consign the bowl for auction tomorrow, she'd have to get it tonight, especially with Hunter lurking about.

Louis, coming from behind Mai, cupped his hand on her elbow. "Angelo has arrived. You must hear all about his marvelous new addition to his draping project, one to die for."

Edna snarled at Walter.

Angelo upstaged Mai as the *artiste de jour*. Ebony curls, olive skin, perfect body. Had he been in the Sistine Chapel he would have hovered around the ceiling with someone's index finger touching him. He wanted eventually to canopy the Venetian canals with bubble wrap *a la* Christo and Jeanne-Claude. But he lacked the lira. So in the meantime he settled for draping the historic Custom House. California was full of wealthy *aficionados* who could sponsor a grand statement of early commerce. Angelo was from Fresno. He knew these things.

And Mai had to admit he was stunning, as always, every bit a star, in a black silk shirt spattered with fuchsia droplets, charcoal slacks, and tan penny loafers. She met his eyes and smiled broadly, no longer mad at him and his big mouth radio interview.

"It's all about cash from the sea, *bella* Mai," Angelo called to her. "A fantasy *molto buono.* The event of the decade. I drape the entire Custom House in a golden dome of billowing cloth with flying sails above it, a representational tall ship, and to view the beautiful gold, I make the camera obscura—

A hideous scream from across the room cut off his sentence.

Heads swooshed away from him.

Another scream.

A shout. "He's not breathing. Call 911!"

Mai held onto Angelo's arm as everyone pressed to the opposite end of the gallery.

"What happened?" the blue-fingered artist asked Mai.

"I can't see," she said.

Angelo elbowed through the pack with Mai still gripping his arm. She felt his arm tense. She released her grip and with both hands turned the shoulders of the man in front of her so she could see.

Walter Elderson, elegant and handsome, lay twisted

in a heap on the floor, motionless. Louis had his fingers on Walter's throat. "There's no pulse," Louis said.

A siren sounded loudly outside the gallery door.

Someone close to Mai said, "He's dead."

Edna frantically searched through her purse. "I can't find Walter's nitroglycerine." She stammered. "He forgot to give it to me. I always carry it for him."

The crowd moved aside so the paramedics could get through.

Helen took Edna's hand. "Come away. There's nothing you can do. He's not breathing."

"He's had a heart attack. Everyone get back," Louis shouted. "In fact, everyone please, please, leave."

Mai circled her arm around Angelo's waist. "Let's go. It's too late. Nothing will help."

Mai pulled Angelo outside, around the corner of the gallery, and up the stairs to his studio.

Once inside, trying not to sound hurried or insensitive, she asked, "Are you okay?"

"Not sure." His voice sounded far away, as if it had traveled through dense fog. He leaned against the kitchen counter.

"I'm sorry about Walter." She hugged him, briefly, then stood at arm's length and looked directly at him. "Can you focus for a few minutes on an urgent problem?"

He looked startled. "Urgent problem?"

Ice replaced the fog in his voice. "Walter is dead down there."

"Oh, Angelo, I am sorry. Truly. You know I am." She should say no more. Get to Elderson's. Find the bowl by herself if she could. But she heard again her grandfather's question on her cell phone in Portsmouth Square, "Mai, are we still connected?" She had to get Walter's bowl for her grandfather. She was afraid Hunter might already be at Elderson's mansion. She spoke very softly.

"I am in trouble. I need your help."

He slumped against the counter, maybe listening, maybe not.

She pretended he had nodded. "You saw the bouquet of sweet flag in the gallery. It's from Hunter. The sweet flag is his 'I'm here ahead of you' taunt. He's going to steal Walter's bowl."

Angelo held the counter with both hands and took a deep breath. When he exhaled, his chest caved into the fuchsia spatters on his silk shirt.

Mai went to the window and looked at the confusion below as the gallery emptied and fancy clothes moved to the side of the ambulance parked below. She had to act in this narrow window of opportunity before Edna returned home.

Angelo sat down on the futon and pressed his head in his hands. "God," he said quietly.

Mai knelt on one knee in front of him. "Listen to me. There is no easy way to say this. I have to get Walter's bowl tonight."

He dropped his hands. "Now? I don't believe you."

Mai raced on through his angry tone. "You do believe me. You know me. Sometimes there isn't a right time to act."

"So Interpol trumps a friend?" Ice. He stood and stepped around her and walked to the front window.

She didn't mean to dismiss his feelings. She followed him as far as the kitchen table but stopped. She closed the David Hockney book that lay open on it and poured the cup of cold coffee into the sink. She had to move on no matter what.

"It's not Interpol. This time it's personal."

"Personal?"

She let his challenging tone roll off and stood beside him at the window, her palm in his, closing her fingers tightly. Her words rushed on.

"This time it is very personal. Believe me. Trust me."

Red lights twirled on the ambulance below. Voices twirled with them. The paramedics loaded the covered body into the ambulance. If Angelo had any hope that Walter might be revived, it surely vanished then.

Mai pressed on, even though she sounded hurried and insensitive. "I have to steal the bowl tonight, with or without your help. That bowl belongs elsewhere. Hunter will get it if I don't. Or Edna will consign it tomorrow. Or Toni will buy it back. Or Helen will talk Edna out of it."

He put his forehead on the window pane, staring directly down at the ambulance.

She gripped his hand with unmistakable urgency. "Angelo?"

He turned from the window. "Everything is suddenly upside down."

"Yes. Everything has changed."

She was angry with herself for not allowing him time to deal with this. As much for herself as for him, she put her arms around him and held him tight, breathing steadily to calm him. Finally, after a long twenty seconds, each breath that he took joined each one of hers in a single rhythm. Something had resolved for him. Then he pulled away.

With his back to the window, to the swirling red lights and to Walter Elderson, Angelo straightened a bit, the fuchsia spatters on his silk shirt expanded. He spread his hands in resignation.

"So." He paused. "We must go forward in an upside down world." He stepped away from the window. "I do know you, Mai Ling. The bowl must be extremely important to you. What do you need?"

She touched his arm. "I wish I didn't have to ask."

"Go ahead."

"Get me something to wear and tell me exactly where Walter kept the bowl."

He went to his closet and found her a black shirt, a pair of navy blue drawstring pants, and some black high top tennis shoes. She unbuttoned her mandarin collar and all the diagonal buttons on her dress and slipped out of it. She hung it up in the closet and put her peacock necklace on the window sill. While Angelo talked, she dressed in his clothes.

"Drive by Walter's house to the alley," Angelo said. "Turn left. Go up halfway. Park on the wrong side as close to the left eugenia hedge as you can. There's a gate into the yard."

He picked up a key from his easel shelf.

"Use this in the kitchen door. Go left through the kitchen to the hallway. Pass the library. Keep going to the first staircase in the foyer. The bowl is in a glass case in his gallery on the second floor. Turn right. Go down the hall to the first door on the left side."

He faded out. His lips scowled.

Mai urged him to continue. "Don't drift away from me now."

He crossed to the futon. "I'm okay." From under the futon he pulled a flashlight and stuffed it in the tote bag he also dragged out. "Don't turn on lights in his gallery.

There are tricky alarms connected to them."

Mai knelt to put on the tennis shoes. "Are you sure you don't have socks? These are way too big." She wrapped the laces around the tops of the shoes before tying them in front.

When she stood, he handed her a black silk scarf. "Put your hair up." As she gathered her hair and tied the scarf tightly around her head, she walked to the window. Eerie orange and yellow colors from the tiki torches hopped around the metallic ambulance doors. Edna talked to the paramedics.

Angelo distractedly folded the cloth tote bag in a small bundle around the flashlight and put it under Mai's arm.

When the ambulance slowly drove away, Mai stepped outside. Angelo whispered one more thing. "Walter's gallery has a punch code lock on the door, 662278 for MOAART, Museum of Ancient Art."

She gave him a look that said "you must be kidding," but then realized it was no time to joke. She whispered, "I am sorry about Walter."

She crept down, not as silently as she hoped because the too big shoes slapped on each step. She stopped at the bottom of the stairs and listened to Edna's tight voice.

"Louis, please, get me out of here."

"Take my arm, dear."

An urgent Robert Giles-Smyth called, "Helen, wait up. I need a ride."

Watching from the shadows until she was sure that none of the four would notice her, Mai moved quickly by the empty tables being bussed in Coconut Café, the bobbing green light on the Harbor Cruise boat's flag, and the picturesque seagulls roosting on the railings. The blue neon Clam Chowder sign in Bernie's window glowed and the purple bulb nose of the ice cream clown, still on battery power, twinkled. It chuckled as Louis, Edna, Helen, and Robert walked by. "Ho. Ho. Ho." She climbed between the clown and the wall so as not to trigger the laughter again and chance anyone turning to look.

At the end of the wharf the quartet in front of her crossed towards the Maritime Museum's parking. She turned left and sprinted along the marina to the Jaguar as fast as she could in Angelo's shoes. She felt as if all five of them were one storm blowing towards the Pacific Grove mansion.

11

A STORMY MANSION

Hunter figured the mansion would be empty and the Eldersons safely out of the way at Mai's show by nine o'clock. In his suite at the five star Cannery Row hotel, he zipped his black leather jacket over his Hawaiian shirt and tied a maroon bandana around his red hair. Downstairs, he had the valet bring his Harley to the front. The hotel, on the ocean in Cannery Row, was less than a mile from Elderson's.

When he got to the mansion, thin fog blurred the few cars that rumbled along in front of it. He turned up the side alley and stopped just short of the back street. After hiding the bike on the right in the eugenia tunnel, he trotted along the street to the service access driveway and turned down it.

A light haloed above a door facing the alley, so he sneaked to the darker, longer, back of the house. That afternoon when he delivered the two jade Buddhas, Walter showed him the covered veranda and camellia and rhododendron garden as well as the rooms downstairs, but not the upstairs.

As he followed the path along the veranda, he rapidly ticked off what he remembered was inside. Just inside the door, a Chippendale dining set. In a cabinet, rare white and blue Chinese dishes from the Kangxi Period, probably 1700 CE. On the wall, Mai Ling's hanging scroll of boats in Three Gorges. The adjoining room was a sitting room with a settee in blue silk and on the wall above it, a portrait of a Gilded Age socialite, 1903, by John Singer Sargent.

The lock on the veranda door was tricky, no question, but he could pick it. Then he'd have less than a minute to run through the dining room to the sitting room, around to the living room and foyer to disable the security alarm. It was a challenge worthy of his skill. He pulled a short wire from a channel in his belt and inserted it in the lock.

Mai switched off the Jaguar's headlights before she turned up the alley. As she drove as far to the left as she could, the car scraped against thick eugenia branches, probably ruining the blue paint on her fender.

She stopped halfway up the alley, so close to the fat eugenia trunks that she could not open her door. She crawled over the gearshift, grabbed the tote bag, and got out the passenger door. A car's headlight traveling on the back street reflected off the gas tank of a Harley jammed against the opposite hedge.

Crap. She knew that idiot would try to steal the bowl tonight.

She reached into the glove compartment, removed her sharp hunting knife from its stiff leather sheath, and expertly slashed both his bike tires. After she jolted the wooden gate open, she stuffed the knife into the tote bag.

A light glowed in the fog over the kitchen door. She ignored it and walked quickly, although not silently, towards the light with Angelo's key in her hand, his shoes slapping on the stone path.

The shoe boats had to go. She sat down, snapped the laces untied, yanked the shoes off and jammed them in the bag. Standing barefoot with the tote bag tucked under her arm, she inserted the key in the lock.

Louis and Edna arrived in front. He parked Elderson's Mercedes in the circular driveway, came around the car, and opened the door for Edna. They were on the porch when Helen and Robert pulled into the driveway in her Toyota.

Edna, too drunk to function well, fumbled in her purse for her key, finally pulled it out, but couldn't steady her shaking hand to get it in the lock.

"Let me do that, dear," Louis said.

Inside, Edna automatically punched four numbers on the security key pad, disabling the alarm and turning on all the inside lights.

Hunter jerked in surprise when the lights came on as he pulled the veranda door shut. Geez. What was this all about?

Mai jumped when the lights came on as she pulled the kitchen door shut. Damn. Edna was here already.

"I'll go make coffee," Louis said, after Edna sat down in a Queen Anne chair in the living room. "Helen, you and Robert stay here with her." He headed to the kitchen by way of the sitting room.

Hunter tiptoed past the Chippendale dining table, keeping the heels of his cowboy boots high so he didn't click along the hardwood floor.

Mai walked silently on her bare feet to the left across the kitchen and peered down the hallway and beyond the staircases to the living room where Helen and Robert sat on a long red velvet sofa with their backs to her. She couldn't see Edna. She ran down the hallway to the first door and slipped into the library. She closed the door.

Hunter, still tiptoeing, crossed the kitchen and leaned his

head into the doorway so that just one eye peeked down the hall. Seeing two heads above the back of a red sofa, he sped on his toes past the library to the staircase, climbed three steps at a time, and hid in the first room he came to, a bedroom. A master bedroom. With balcony. He crept onto the balcony and stared down at the Mercedes and Toyota. What the hell was going on? Mai's show should still be in full swing. He hurried back inside and surveyed the room. Louis XIV furniture. Several large dressers. Ornate bed. A dozen pictures on the walls, none that he wanted, except maybe the small watercolor of the Pont Neuf. He searched for a safe that might hide the bowl.

Mai heard things happening in the kitchen. She waited. She smelled coffee. She watched from the slightly opened library door while Louis carried a tray of cups and a pot of coffee down the hall. When he reached the living room, she sidestepped along the hall wall to the staircase. She climbed three steps at a time to the top.

Hunter came out of the bedroom.

In the living room, Edna noticed, without caring, that Louis placed a tray on the low mahogany table and distributed coffee. She was not sober, nor did she want to be. She wasn't sure how she was feeling, empty maybe. Not a lot different from how she'd felt for a long time. Thirty years ago, when she married Walter, love was what she felt. She came to their marriage with wealth, social standing, and the inheritance of her father's precious art collection. But what she treasured most in those early years was Walter. What sustained her through the unsettling times of his self-centered success and numerous affairs was the memory of the young man she loved. As the years went by, that memory faded. She had more and more difficulty forgiving his frequent infidelities, coping in private with feelings of betrayal and rejection while in public pretending a stoic indifference. Still, hidden away, deep inside her, was the young man from the past. Until he became infatuated with Angelo. Tonight at Coconut Gallery when for the first time she saw Angelo in the same room with Walter, emotions which she could not control completely emptied her. Her young man vanished. Walter died, even before he died. The coffee was too bitter to drink.

Louis sipped his cupful as he looked around the room. He would miss Walter Elderson, his cash cow. He'd sold Walter the yellow Chihuly glass bowl on the coffee table, Mai's hanging scroll of the Three Gorges in the dining room, and the Taos Pueblo pottery jar by the fireplace. He sighed between sips.

Robert stirred three spoons of sugar and half of the small pitcher of cream into his coffee. He would miss the access to society that he was privy to because of the Eldersons' bent for publicizing each new art acquisitions. Generally, however, he felt happy. He had a good story to write for tomorrow's *Art Wise Press.* And new alliances.

Helen held her cup with both hands but did not drink. She preferred tea. She sat back against the red velvet sofa. She would miss absolutely nothing about Walter Elderson and his blatant plan to sell the historic bowl to the highest bidder. Maybe now she could convince Edna to let the university safeguard it.

At the top of the stairs Mai smacked into Hunter. He got her in a headlock and pressed his lips to her ear. "Good evening, Mai. Nice outfit."

She butted the back of her head against his chin so hard that he released his hold. She dropped down out of his arm at the same time kicking her heel into his shin. He grabbed her wrist, spun her around to face him, and pulled the tote bag with both hands.

She let the bag go but pushed it with both palms, hitting his chest with the long flashlight in the bag. She heard air explode from him and jumped backwards. With a kick, she sank her foot into his stomach and knocked him against the tasteful pale green wallpaper. There was a muffled thunk when he landed on the plush carpet.

She dashed through the open bedroom door but Hunter tackled from behind and she fell onto a cool satin bedspread. The deep mattress squished out a startled sigh. She squirmed out of his grasp and rolled toward the pillows but he was instantly on top of her, pinning her to the royal bed. Cheap aftershave, musk or something, reeked on his neck and his strong chest pressed down hard on her breasts.

"Cypress delivered my greeting?" he whispered, his mouth again on her ear.

"You, Cypress, and sweet flag—the devil's triangle," Mai whispered back. Again she butted her head, this time into his nose. He yelped. She twisted onto her side, almost out from under him, but he locked an arm across her chest.

"Evil little foxes shouldn't preach about the devil," he said nasally but quietly.

"I didn't see your white steed in the hallway," she said. With a free hand she bent his fingers back to his wrist, broke away, and crawled off the bed. A heavy crystal figurine sat on the bedside table. She threw it at him. He blocked it with a pillow just as a second object, a hardback book, clunked into the figurine.

"Keep making nasty noises and we'll have company from downstairs," he said, and tossed aside the pillow, struggling to sit up.

She heaved the clock radio. Its electrical cord pulled the bedside lamp over. He caught the radio, instantly dropped it on the mattress, and bent half off the bed to catch the lamp. As he dangled there, lamp in hand, she pulled the satin spread up from the foot of the bed and wrapped it around him and the lamp.

"Nighty-night," she cooed.

In three giant strides she reached the tote bag in the

hallway and snatched it up. With two more strides she faced Elderson's gallery door. She punched 662278 on the door's keypad and heard the bolt slide just as she saw Hunter stumble out of the bedroom door. She pushed the door open enough to get around it. Inside, she leaned against the door to close it. She felt resistance. When she heard Hunter hiss, "shhhhit," she slammed her hip and shoulder hard against the door and forced it shut.

12

THE DARK CHAMBER

In the totally dark chamber she got out the flashlight and scanned the room. The beam landed on the glass case across the room. She dodged a snaky-haired female hovering over a reading chair and came eye to eye with a harpy next to the case. "Such taste," she said out loud.

On the top shelf of the case, a Japanese shadow puppet stood next to a small, square, Mayan stone glyph. On the middle shelf was an elaborate gold necklace, probably from a tomb in the Valley of the Kings. And there, on the bottom shelf, two eight inch jade Buddhas meditated on either side of an empty space.

Her whole body lost control. She fell against the harpy. "No," she said. "It can't be gone." She was not talking quietly. She spun around, searching the room with the flashlight beam. Hunter could not possibly have gotten in here. He wouldn't have yanked the tote bag out of her hand if he had the bowl.

She threw herself down in the chair under the wings of Medusa, angry and breathing hard. She had Angelo's insider information. How could something so easy go wrong?

She had to calm down, look around.

The flashlight beam landed on a packing crate. Maybe Walter stashed the bowl there. She slid out of the chair and crawled to the crate. The pictures in it were tight. She put the flashlight on the floor and pulled one out to make room for her hand. No bowl would fit in there. She stared at the picture as she crammed it back in. Was it bad lighting, or was this the picture Interpol knew had just come out of Paris as a Picasso forgery? At this point, who cared? She glared up at Medusa. Where was the damn bowl? Medusa stared back. No answers there.

Before she opened the door, she turned off the flashlight and put it into the tote bag. When she peered out into the hall, she saw Hunter leaning against the bedroom doorjamb, waiting with bleeding fingers pressed into his floral shirt.

Suddenly she knew why he was waiting with that stupid grin on his face. Footsteps sounded on the stairs along with Helen's voice. "It will only take a moment, Edna. We'll just make sure the bowl is safe."

A wicked smile curled on Hunter's lips. Clearly he waited for her to get caught. He ducked back into the bedroom.

Down the hall from the gallery, away from the staircase, was another door. Mai dashed to it and into another bedroom, luckily, a bedroom with a window to the back of the house. She moved fast. Security lights lit a peacock roosting on a slatted veranda roof. She raised the window and climbed out. As she balanced on the slats, she tossed the tote bag over the roof and heard it clunk on the ground. She reached up and shut the window.

"Help. Help," the peacock cried.

Mai startled. The peacock lumbered towards her, dragging its huge tail with a ratcheting sound across the slats. "Angelo didn't tell me about you," she whispered, and caught its neck with one hand and pinched its beak shut with the other. "Scoot," she said. "And keep quiet."

She hit the ground running, scooped up the tote bag, and dashed out the gate to the car. She threw the tote bag on the passenger seat in the Jaguar and crawled over it and the gearshift. Hunter would soon find his bike, flat tires and all.

Without turning on her headlights, she eased the car out of the alley. Turn right? Turn left? She had no idea where to go now, empty handed. And really pissed.

"Help. Help," the peacock cried.

13

SARDINES

The initial shock Angelo felt when Walter died had been tempered by Mai's plea for help. However, when she left, he vacillated wildly between anger at the suddenness of death and a disconnected isolation. He needed to talk to someone. He walked alone down the deserted wharf. Off in the black night a single seal barked from a distant buoy and water slapped against the sides of anchored boats. For the first time since he'd lived here, the wharf seemed ghostly.

He paced along Del Monte Avenue, oblivious to the traffic, not thinking, not feeling, until he found himself in the midst of a Cannery Row crowd pushing into Sardines, a jazz club. He rubbed his head, trying to orient himself. Sardines was a good place to be. He needed a drink. And Tuck and Patti were listed on the What's Happening sign in front.

Sardines was packed. Angelo nudged his way into the bar area of the performance space, reassured a little by the odd mixture of elegance and crap which its owner, Max, had assembled. The metal and brick walls were bleak, the lighting exquisite.

"Angelo," Max called. "Good to see you." He put his arm around Angelo's shoulders, snapping his fingers at the bartender. "Get Angelo whatever he wants."

"A brandy, thanks." Angelo watched the reds, violets, and yellows pouring from the ceiling's backlit replica of Notre Dame's Rose Window. Colors swirled on the bar, his brandy glass, every face, changing directions like a darting school of sardines.

"I'll fit a table in by the stage," Max said. Angelo carried his drink past twenty tables with twenty candles flickering yellow and dripping wax onto vintage Chianti bottles. Max repositioned a table and two teak chairs for the best view of the stage.

"Aren't these great chairs?" Max shouted over the noise. "I got such a deal in Bombay."

"Absolutely," Angelo hollered back. "Bollywood to perfection." He squeezed into the chair and put the brandy on the table. "They add to the charm of that ornate staircase as it ascends to escape cholera from stage right to stage left."

Max patted his shoulder. "Love ya, too, Angelo. Enjoy."

Angelo felt himself slide into sensory overload.

Tuck and Patti came onstage.

Angelo listened to the intricate guitar music of Tuck and the soft vocal melodies of Patti. They finished the set with "Castles Made of Sand."

When the song ended, Max brought another brandy and pulled up a chair. "Ready for your big event on Saturday?"

"Getting there."

"I just heard about Walter. What can I say? I'm sorry."

Angelo nodded.

Max looked over Angelo's shoulder and stood but put one palm on the table and one on Angelo's shoulder. He leaned down close. "The side door is unlocked if you want to escape. Cypress de la Mer just floated in."

"Cypress de la Mer? The woman known as *mal de mer*?"

"Yep."

"The woman who consumes sweet flag all day long?"

"Yep."

"The woman I'm married to?"

"The very one. And heading this way."

Angelo gulped some brandy and turned.

Cypress's soft white dress dipped low on her breasts, clung gently to her waist, and danced around her body's curves. As she moved towards him, the colors of the Rose Window splashed on her pale form. The white, the colors. She was a spectacular ghost.

So lovely.

With his foot Angelo scooted a chair out for her.

She looked around as if checking for someone. "I didn't expect to see you, Angelo. Why aren't you at Coconut for Mai Ling's gala?"

"Been there." He studied her scraped cheek and the gash on her forehead. Old worries surfaced. "What happened to your face?"

"A heated disagreement over art with Walter Elderson. I can't understand what you find worthwhile in him."

Angelo moved the Chianti candle to the side so he could see her without the flame's shadow-play on her face. He signaled the waiter. "What were you doing at Walter's this afternoon?" He wasn't sure he wanted an answer.

"Planting and purchasing."

A flash of dread swept through him.

The waiter came. She ordered scotch and soda. Her words slurred.

His old protective habit kicked in. "Have coffee with me, Cypress. I've had too much brandy. Two coffees," he said to the waiter.

He chose his next words carefully. His castles made of sand had begun to crumble in the tide of Walter's death. Now fear lapped against castle walls as the image of Walter naked at the top of the stairs in the lingering aroma of sweet flag sprang into his head. Cypress and Walter were not two he wanted paired in any way. "You bought something from Walter this afternoon?"

"In a manner of speaking."

"In what manner?" Flashing colors, flickering candles, noise, grief, suspicion. It was too much. Angelo erupted. "Walter had a heart attack. He died at Coconut."

Cypress stared at him. Then shrugged. "Can't say I care. The bastard tried to kill me."

"What the hell does that mean? For a change, Cypress, be someone who makes sense."

The waiter put two coffee mugs on the table.

She glared. "Right. You are Mister Sensible at all times." She sipped the coffee. But then her voice and her eyes softened. "Sorry."

"I'm sorry, too." He really was strung out. The coffee burned his tongue. He swallowed hard.

Cypress leaned towards him and confided. "Walter and I negotiated a trade for that Chinese bronze bowl. When I got as far as the koi pond with it, he charged from behind and knocked the bowl into the pond. I hit him. He threw me down. When I came to, I saw the glass door into the library wasn't shut. I went in and up the stairs. I heard Edna shouting in the bedroom. His gallery door wasn't shut either so I helped myself."

The candle sputtered. The tide peaked. Turrets collapsed. "You took the Chinese bronze bowl?" Angelo said, barely.

"Lord. You do need coffee. Aren't you listening to me?" She took another drink of coffee. "Yes, I took it. He had it. I got it. He got it back. I got it. Now it's gone."

To applause, Tuck and Patti returned to the stage. Angelo raised his voice over the clapping. "What do you mean it's gone? Where is the bowl now?"

"Sold. Why?"

He pressed his palms into his eye sockets. Mai never lost an artifact she went after. She wanted this one for some intense personal reason that he didn't understand. "Who did you sell it to?"

"Why do you care? What's going on? You never get attached to objects." She leaned back in the chair and gave him a knowing look. "That's why you make art that only lasts for days."

"Like relationships."

"Like life." Now her voice was barely audible.

She was right. Whether he created art, a relationship, or a life, they were all castles made of sand.

Tuck and Patti overwhelmed him. He couldn't see the swirling colors anymore. He couldn't hear the music anymore. He couldn't feel any more.

He stared at the coffee cup.

"Things can't be that bad," Cypress said. "You manage."

"Like hell."

He swallowed more hot coffee and remembered

Mai's plea for his help. He reached out, touched Cypress's arm, and lied. "It's just that the bowl is important to me. I'm making a camera obscura because of it. I had plans."

"So did half a dozen others. Like my dinner date who stood me up."

Angelo could barely hear Cypress over the music.

He pulled her shoulders close. "Just tell me who has it. Maybe I can buy it back."

"It's too late. Besides, I don't believe you. You're up to something else." Abruptly, she pushed the chair backwards. "I have to go buy my own dinner."

She crossed in front of the stage and disappeared in the standing-room-only crowd. Angelo sank down into the teak Bollywood chair, feeling waves wash away his life, watching cholera come down that ornate stage staircase towards him.

14

FLOWERS FOR SPECIAL OCCASIONS

As soon as she got inside her Casa Munras room, Mai threw Angelo's borrowed clothes on the bed and pulled on her own jeans, an otter t-shirt, and tennis shoes that fit. By now, the empty space between two Buddhas must have jolted Helen, Edna, Robert, and Louis as much as it had her. Edna and Robert would be happy to point a finger at Angelo. She had to warn him.

With any luck, Hunter was still trapped in Edna's bedroom. But her luck wasn't so hot tonight, so just in case he managed to get new tires in the middle of the night and came searching for her car, she left the Jaguar parked by her room. Let him think she was in for the night.

She jogged down Alvarado and into the English pub. "Have you seen Angelo tonight, Charles?"

"Not since this afternoon when he buzzed in for a couple of minutes to talk with three frazzled construction workers. Try Sardines. For some odd reason, he likes that place."

She ran down the deserted wharf and up the stairs to

Angelo's, hoping she'd find him there. She didn't. Guilt tightened her stomach. She had not been very sympathetic. She was worried.

David Hockney's book was still on the kitchen table. She tapped the cover. Hockney's theory that camera obscura images projected on canvas were traced by Old Masters was exciting. But for Angelo and her, an upside down, inverted image on a Zhou Dynasty bowl was big trouble. Maybe the bronze was, as Helen proclaimed, the lost bowl of a Zhou king. Now, damn it, it was lost again.

She found Angelo's car keys on the easel. Wherever he was, he was walking. She'd drive his Jeep to Sardines to look for him. Before she got to the door, she saw Louis walk by the corner window. In a mad dash, she grabbed a kimono from the closet, wrapped it around her jeans and t-shirt, and opened the door before he got to it.

"Louis. Is Edna all right?"

"Good heavens, dear, you startled me. Whatever are you doing here this time of night?"

"I'm fixing tea, waiting for Angelo. He's very upset. What are you doing here?"

"Actually, I came looking for Angelo. I thought he might know the whereabouts of the Chinese bowl. It's missing from Walter's gallery. Edna is accusing him of stealing it." He stepped into the studio, glancing around.

"Really?" She usually played innocent without any telltale sign, but her cheeks warmed, so she repeated her question. "How is Edna?"

"Not thinking clearly, I'm afraid. Helen, Robert, and I tried to console her. She was shocked and distressed by Walter's death, of course. She seemed to be handling it as well as could be expected until she had that second shock, poor dear. She and Helen discovered the bowl was missing. Both became hysterical. Terrible thing. It pushed her into a nasty, violent rage. Says Angelo is to blame for everything. Started drinking. Very upsetting. Made us leave."

He shifted his feet, backing to the door. "I wish Angelo were here." He looked around the room one more time before closing the door.

In the minute she had to wait for Louis to get off the wharf, she paced, too anxious to sit still. She picked up the phone and called Sardines.

"Max, by any chance is Angelo there?"

"Indeed he is, Mai. Can you come get him? He doesn't look so good."

Mai drove Angelo's Jeep to Cannery Row and inched her way through the crowded street. Angelo waved to her and scrambled down the street towards the Jeep, touching fenders, jumping out of the way of the cars. Without waiting for Mai to stop, he pulled the door open and climbed in.

"Cypress had the bowl. It might still be in her shop. If not, she always tracks her sales somehow. Drive to Carmel."

"What?" She wasn't expecting that. Her eyes widened. "Are you sure?"

He gave Mai a quick summary of the Cypress encounter.

Mai listened intently, encouraged that it was Cypress, not someone unknown, who had the bowl. She weighed possibilities as he spoke, hearing fatigue and sadness in his voice. She didn't have the heart to tell him that Louis came looking for him. "Are you okay?"

"I'll get a second wind," Angelo said. "Tell me what

happened at Walter's."

Mai talked fast and drove faster, stress creeping into her voice and tightening her chest. The night was ticking away. She wanted that bowl.

After midnight Carmel was tucked in. As Mai eased the Jeep down the hill towards Carmel Floral Treasures, the only light she saw came from Art Wise Press. Robert was probably banging out a story with all the gritty details of Walter's death for tomorrow's paper.

Angelo took a key ring from the glove compartment. "Better not park here. Go round to the back. We can get in the workroom door. Her van should be parked back there. You check the van, I'll check her safe."

Angelo left the workroom door open so he could see by the light from the outside security spot. On his way to the office safe, he searched a jumble of long white flower boxes, green tissue paper, brown twine, purple and yellow ribbon, and dug his hands into the potting soil in low bins. He found nothing. He crossed to the cuckoo clock by Cypress's office door and slid open the tiny drawer under the cuckoo, took out a little silver key on a long blue ribbon, and turned the lock in the office door.

Since the light in the office would not be visible from the street, he flipped the switch on and saw, as he knew he would, a large painting hanging on the wall, the last painting Cypress ever made, a watercolor of The Lone Cypress.

Staring at the picture, he closed his fist around the silver key, deeply sad. In Sardines, the death of Walter mingled with the ghost of Cypress. Then on the wild Jeep ride to Carmel a long buried emotion bounced up, his desire to be with Cypress the way they had been an eternity ago. That past, however, grew distorted like the lone cypress tree, twisted by too many strong winds. And Cypress herself became that struggling tree, barely surviving.

Angelo took down the painting, propped it against the wall, and spun the combination of the wall safe. In it he found a stack of order forms bound by a rubber band. He quickly flipped through them. They were customer forms, like the ones he could see spread out on her desk. He went to the desk and compared them. The desk forms had customer names which he recognized. The safe forms had only initials. The wad in the safe differed, as far as he could tell, only in that respect. He felt a shooting pain in his stomach. If Cypress already sold the bowl, nothing here would help them find it.

Mai ran her hand the length of Cypress's van, grasped the double side door handle and eased it up and down a couple of times. She pressed it up hard and yanked. It opened. Cypress moved treasures in this van. There had to be a secret compartment. A few twigs and leaves littered the floor and two tubs of sticks and thistles were pushed against the rear window.

Mai climbed onto the driver's bucket seat. She felt under both seats and in the glove compartment. She pressed her palms against the headliner, checking for bumps or anything like a hidden cache. Finding nothing, she sat cross-legged in the back of the van and drummed her fingers along the side paneling. The paneling under the rear window bulged and the carpet didn't fit against the wall neatly. She moved the tubs of sticks and thistles out of the way and wiggled her fingers under the paneling. The whole length lifted out, leaving a space about one inch wide into which an extremely thin artifact might fit, maybe a bug or two.

But not a bowl.

She fit the paneling back in. Where to look next?

She gripped the cool rims of the tubs to slide them back in place and suddenly remembered one of her grandfather's maxims.

Never neglect the obvious.

She dumped tall eucalyptus sticks out of one tub, kept one arm in the tub and estimated the thickness of the bottom, which was normal. She did the same for the tub of thistles. Her hand inside the tub stopped three quarters of the way down so she pressed the bottom plastic. It tilted up.

Bingo.

She felt paper. Damn. She sat back on her heels and took a few long breaths. It was only an envelope. She hurried inside.

"Find anything in the safe?" Mai asked Angelo who stood at the desk reading forms.

"Not really."

"I found only this in the van." Mai tore the envelope opened. It was some sort of accounting sheet, notations of sums paid to Walter Elderson by Wilson Imports.

Angelo read over her shoulder. "Why would Cypress have this?"

"I don't know. Walter should have paid Wilson Imports, not the other way around. I'll figure it out later." She stuffed the sheet into her back pocket. Her chest thumped. She rubbed the back of her neck. Had she been hunting the bowl for Interpol, she would have walked away and tried later. Artifacts had a way of turning up again and again. She could wait to try later with an impersonal challenge. But not this one.

The cuckoo clock sang a single note. With a definite edge in her voice, she said, "It's one in the morning already. That bowl is probably on its way out of California."

"Hold on. Don't give up," Angelo said, as if responding to Mai's frustration. "There must be something here. Something obvious. Cypress hides things in obvious spots. And she keeps records of everything. I did find these in the safe."

He handed her the stack of order forms.

"Okay," she said. "We have nothing else. These were in the safe for a reason." She spread them one by one on the desk. "What's odd about them?"

"They only have initials for customer names."

"And," she said, "they are all C.O.D. orders, this one for Windsor Tea, this for Silver Jubilee, this for Sutter's Gold. Angelo, these are all roses."

"They can't be. Cypress doesn't sell roses."

She pointed to forms. "Well, Olympiad, Tiffany, and McGredy's Ivory are."

"Roses?"

"Definitely." Mai lined the forms on the desk side by side. "She's doing something with roses. Hang on. Find the Olympiad order again. What's the date?"

He sorted through the array. "Here it is. April, this year."

"All right." She put her hands on her hips. "I've got

what she's doing. A silver brooch with the likeness of the goddess Hera on Olympus came out of Greece and on the market in California in April."

She picked up another form. "And Sutter's Gold is the name for pieces from Turkey with no known provenance."

"That's it. She knows what she sells by naming it for a rose," Angelo said.

"Find today's orders," Mai said, her voice tense again.

"They might be on the counter out front." He rushed through the beaded curtain, grabbed four forms off the counter, and rushed back. "Here," he said, "C.O.D., Flamingo Garden's Tea, ordered by BTC. BTC. That's Robert Giles-Smyth, Bob-The-Critic."

She read it quickly. "Only he didn't order Flamingo Garden's Tea roses. He ordered a peacock's garden on a Chinese bronze bowl."

"Holy crap." He slapped the form down on the counter. "Where would he get that kind of money and what did he do with the bowl?"

"Let's find out. Maybe we can catch him at Art Wise Press."

In quick succession, Mai put the rose orders back in the safe, Angelo rehung the painting, and they tore out of Carmel Floral Treasures.

"Wait." Mai stopped Angelo's hand before he turned the Jeep's ignition key. "Everyone knows your Jeep. We'd better try Art Wise Press on foot."

"Carmel is in for the night. No one will see us."

"Maybe not. But I don't want the blame for anything else coming your way."

"Anything else?"

She sprinted away without explaining. As they crashed out onto the street, headlights beamed at them. They squashed back against a wall. Two cars passed slowly by, radios blaring.

"Great. Beach partiers." Angelo said. "They'll wake the dead."

They stood absolutely still until the music died away. Then they took off across the small patio of Swiss Café Chocolates and into the parking spaces next to Art Wise Press. Angelo stopped abruptly. Mai plowed into his back.

"What?" she whispered.

"There's a car in front of Art Wise."

"Wait."

The light went out in Art Wise Press. Bob-The-Critic came out and got into the car.

Mai grabbed Angelo's sleeve. "We can't get to the Jeep in time to follow them."

"No," Angelo said. "But if they're headed to Bob's, we can get there on foot. It's just down the hill by the ocean."

"Go. I'm right behind."

15

COTTAGES BY THE SEA

Mai and Angelo arrived, chests heaving, at the east side of Bob-The-Critic's secluded Carmel cottage. A smattering of moonlight filtered through the canopy of trees. The same car they had seen in front of Art Wise Press was parked on the street parallel to the entry porch and a stone's throw away. They crouched between the hydrangea bushes at the corner of the small porch.

Mai's hand on Angelo's chest told him to stay put. She groped along the side of the house and peered under the bottom slat of a closed Venetian blind. She could see nothing. At the next window, shadow figures moved on the lace drapery. She crept back to Angelo.

"I can't see anything. We have to get them to come out," she whispered. "Go around to the other side of the car and bump it."

"Why?"

"Set off the car alarm. Then run. Someone will come out," she said.

"That's not much of a plan."

"It's all I've got. When someone comes out, I'm going in."

"That really is not much of a plan."

"Just do it," she said.

Angelo crawled out of the bushes and scurried to the far side of the car. Seconds later, the car alarm shrieked.

The front door opened. Bob's poodle bolted out, yipping wildly, followed instantly by Frank Conti.

Mai shuddered. Frank Conti. The real enemy. Robert was just a go-between and a flake. She could handle him. But Conti. Big problem.

Frank stood at the edge of the porch and pointed the remote at the car.

The car shut up. The dog didn't. Yip. Yap. Yip. Yip.

"See anything?" Bob asked from the doorway.

"No. Get the damn dog." Frank looked up and down the street.

"Maybe a cat pounced on the hood," Bob said. "Napoleon. Napoleon. Come here," Bob called quietly. Napoleon let out a sharp cry from the other side of the car. Bob swooped around the trunk and emerged with the wiggling animal in his arms.

The alarm shrieked again.

Mai jumped. Angelo was still somewhere by the car.

"Turn it off," Bob yelled over the yipping.

Pointing the remote again, Frank stepped off the porch.

With no one between her and the door, Mai bolted over the porch railing into the house and shut the door with a quiet click.

She dashed through the cottage to the room where

she'd seen the shadows on the lace curtain. On a dining table was a packing box with a Wilson Imports label and FRAGILE MUSEUM PIECE stamped across the side. Next to it were scissors and tape. In a crystal ashtray, a cigarette burned.

Mai heard the front door rattle and Conti shout, "Robert, how the hell did the door shut? You'd better have your key."

"One is hidden on the back porch," Bob said, slightly louder than Napoleon's continued yipping.

Mai scooped the box into her arms and crouched under the table, out of sight of the window which Bob would pass on the way to the back of the house.

Packing tape stuck the lid down tight. She crawled her fingers along the table top to the scissors, snagged them, and with a quick slice had the tape off. When she pulled shredded packing paper out, her knuckles hit a hard shape. She pulled it out of the box.

"Thank God," she said, moving her finger around the rim in a gesture of intimate relief which lasted half a second. She heard the lock turn in the back door. With both hands she refilled the box with the packing paper. She stood, put the box on the table, plucked the burning cigarette from the ashtray and dropped it in the box. Smoke curled up. The back door opened.

She scooped up the bowl and, as she fled to the front door, anchored it under her t-shirt on her stomach in case she needed two hands for whatever occurred next. She opened the door. Frank, bent at the waist, was half in, half out of the car, his head under the dash, apparently looking for a loose wire or some reason why the alarm kept sounding.

Mai vaulted over the porch railing and dropped behind the hydrangea bush onto a coiled garden hose. She stepped off the hose and planted her feet on solid ground, ready for anything.

"Fire," Bob yelled. "Fire." He barreled onto the porch in a stink of smoke, shrieking in a high pitched voice, "The bowl's on fire!"

Yip. Yip. Yip. Napoleon's barks echoed Bob in the same grating pitch.

Mai stretched her hand under the railing, caught Bob's moving pant leg, and sent him staggering down the steps with uncontrolled forward momentum which ceased when he splayed across the hood of the car, head and arms dangling over the front headlight.

Frank jumped out of the car, leaving the door ajar. Napoleon's frantic little paws clambered into the car, over the front seat into the back, then over again into the front. Frank grabbed Bob's legs and tried to pull him off the car.

But the car moved forward a fraction of an inch, then an inch, then two inches, slowly coasting down the lonely road towards the sea. Napoleon bailed.

Uh-oh. Small problem.

Mai could see Angelo's head on the uphill pavement under the car, revealed inch by inch as the car picked up speed. Napoleon saw it too. He wagged and snipped and sunk his teeth into Angelo's hair and pulled hard.

The stink of smoke around the porch indicated that the fire had reached the varnish on the dining room table. The car moved onward down the hill. Taking hurried steps to keep up with the car, Frank managed to pull Bob off the car and together they landed flat on the ground. The car smashed to a halt, its hood embedded in one of

Carmel's invincible pines.

Mai found the water faucet, turned it full on, aimed the power nozzle at Napoleon, and squeezed. The shot of water knocked the frantic dog off Angelo and all the way across the street.

Mai hurled the hose as hard as she could. It thrashed, flopped, twisted, and spewed water over house, car, street, and the heap that was Bob and Frank.

"Son of a bitch," Frank yelled. He jumped up and ran downhill to get out of range. Bob covered his head with his hands.

Under the dark canopy of trees, Mai and Angelo took off. They dodged the soggy body of Napoleon and made it through a hedge and over two low fences. Then, in a tree enshrouded back yard, Angelo collapsed.

"I can't go on," he said, his hands on his knees, his head bent down. "My legs won't move. Too heavy."

Mai wrapped his arm over her shoulder and held him up. He was alarmingly weak. "Rest a minute." She looked around the tiny yard. They couldn't stay here. "Doesn't Cypress live nearby?"

"Two gardens up."

"Then we'll get help from her. Hold on." Still supporting him, she as much as dragged him to Cypress's back door.

"Just open it," Angelo said. "She never locks it."

Inside, he slumped down on the bench in the kitchen nook.

"Quiet," Mai said.

"Just find me some sugar. I'm hypoglycemic, that's all."

She opened the refrigerator, looking for juice or fruit. All she saw was one bunch of carrots with the leaves attached and a whole sunflower.

"There's absolutely nothing here."

She looked at Angelo. In the cold light of the open fridge door, she saw that his hands were bleeding from the bits of road gravel stuck to his palms and his curls glistened from dog saliva and hose spray. His shirt, soaked, stuck to his chest. More guilt knotted her stomach.

The overhead light flicked on. "Don't tell me you've been swimming in the ocean this time of night?" Cypress said from the doorway. She shuffled into the room on Chinese slippers, wearing soft silk pajamas, but there was a hard challenge in her question. "What are you two up to?"

"Cypress, sorry." Angelo rubbed his palms. "We're in a bit of a bind. We'll just be a minute. I need to catch my breath."

"So I see." She picked up his hands. "Blood? It won't come out, you know, Lady Macbeth." She pulled several sheets of paper towels from a roll, wet them under the sink faucet, and handed them to Angelo. She stared at Mai. "Are you pregnant?"

"It looks that way," Mai said and tucked her shirt again around the bowl. She didn't want to admit anything.

Cypress glared. "Is that a million dollar baby you're carrying?"

"Don't ask," Angelo said, patting the blood and soot from his hands.

"Do you have some orange juice or syrup? Something with instant sugar for him?" Mai asked. She wanted quickly to get back to the Jeep and out of Carmel before Frank and Bob recovered. They might begin a search for the bowl with Cypress since she was the one who sold it to Bob. A great weight lurked at the base of Mai's skull. Now there were three of them up to their tails in cold river water because of the little Chinese bowl.

Cypress stirred heaping spoons of sugar into a glass of apple cider. "This will work."

Angelo drank it down. After a minute, he seemed better.

"Eat this as well." Cypress handed him peanut butter and honey on a folded piece of bread.

"I'm sorry we had to sneak in here," Mai said. "I think we can get out now." Angelo rose slowly, clutching the bread.

"Watch out for night creatures," Cypress said.

"You watch out too," Mai said. "I have a bad feeling this isn't over."

After Angelo dropped Mai at Casa Munras, he drove directly to Fisherman's Wharf and climbed his studio stairs, his legs wobbly and his brain foggier than the offshore air. But when he opened his studio door and flipped on the light, his sudden intake of breath jerked him into high alert.

"Now what?" He fell against the door.

His studio was trashed. The easel was a heap of sticks, the futon pad, a hump on the floor. Smears of vermilion oil paint covered his sample bolt of golden nylon which lay unfurled across the futon frame.

"Who the hell moves this fast?"

Paint brushes, dishes, pots, forks, and shards of coffee cups covered the floor. He booted the tea kettle so hard that it bounced off the stove. Then he saw remnants of fabric, rags.

"Not that."

Mai's dress was untouched. But his clothes lay scattered on the floor in front of the closet, ripped to ribbons. Pinned to the closet door by a butcher knife, his favorite plum blossom kimono dangled pathetically, one sleeve hanging by just three silk threads.

When the adrenalin which rushed through his arteries filtered out a little, he picked up a purple collar, a mauve pant leg, a rainbow shirt front. He wiggled loose the butcher knife, letting the kimono slump to the floor.

The rending of clothes was a Biblical activity. Why would someone looking for the bowl need to do it?

Someone looking for the bowl wouldn't.

This was not a search. This was a kill-and-destroy rage. He could almost smell the smoldering cigar smoke of Freud.

No mystery here.

Edna.

THURSDAY

16

THE MORNING AFTER

The sun pushing through the Thursday morning fog cast a muted light which angled into Mai's Casa Munras room through barely open curtains. Mai wasn't ready for full light. Elderson's death, Angelo's distress, her capture of the bowl, a couple hours sleep—her head throbbed.

A few hours ago at Carmel Floral Treasures, she and Angelo surrounded the bowl with moss, stuck it in a hanging basket, and plunked a potted gazania in it. Now, in her slip, two fingers around the basket's hook, she carried it outside. The wisteria vine trellising above the walkway and pink gazanias in a flower box between the parking space and her door shielded her from the parking spaces. She hung the basket among the broad green leaves of the wisteria. A gardener sent by James Chang would pick it up soon.

Her portfolio containing the hungry jays which she had painted yesterday lay on the antiqued white table in front of the window. Most of the portfolio was in shadow, but a thin sliver of light from the gap in the curtains streaked across its center. Yin shadow and yang light. Out of balance. Harmony was beyond her reach.

Yesterday she'd no time for the messy task of pasting the delicate rice paper picture onto firmer mounting paper. She wouldn't have time today either. For Louis's auction at noon, she'd just have to put the picture in a sandwich of mat, glass, and ebony frame which she'd carried in the portfolio. The jays would be smoothed onto mounting paper later as part of the sale. The picture was like her life at the moment, not ideal, but fixable.

She looked out the window. Down the walkway, moving very slowly, a gardener pushed a wheelbarrow. He stopped at the gazania flower box several doors down, pulled a few dead blooms from stalks, and stirred the soil with a hand tool.

Good. He'd be at the hanging basket in front of her door in a minute. She slipped into a hand dyed, seafoam swirl of a silk skirt, buttoned on a white mandarin jacket embroidered diagonally with pink peonies and wandering green leaves, and stuck her feet in sandals. With the strap of a small, red dragon purse over her left shoulder, she lifted the portfolio's leather handle with her right hand and took one step out the door.

Whack.

The jolt from the impact of a hand slammed into her chest caught Mai off guard, but automatically her ribcage moved backward to absorb its force. The hand pressed up to her neck and fingers squeezed her jaw. A familiar voice said, "By rights I should break your pretty neck."

She could see Hunter's other hand, two fingers splinted and swollen.

"Overreacting to pinched fingers?" she said through fixed teeth, glad that she had inflicted some small damage last night.

"Step back inside and don't be cute."

He released her neck and shoved her, grazing the back of his head on the hanging basket. "Ouch. A person has to put up with the stupidest crap to get to you."

"One man's crap is another's treasure." She glanced at the gardener, still one flower box away but approaching fast.

"Oh, sir," the gardener called, "I am so sorry. Are you hurt? Let me take this basket out of your way."

"He deserves to be hurt," Mai said. "Give him the basket. I only wish it contained belladonna."

"Your poison way of saying 'I love you' no doubt," Hunter said, pushing the basket aside as the gardener offered it to him.

"Hardly. 'Get lost' would be more like it," Mai said. Inside, she dropped the portfolio and purse on the small chair and sat on the edge of the window table in a nonchalant pose, although her fight mode had kicked in, as it usually did when she vied with him for an artifact. "I could actually have Cypress send belladonna to you for your injured hand."

"Still harping on deadly nightshade, are you?" Hunter shut the door. "That poison might work on you. Foxbane sure as hell doesn't, not, at least, in the form of Cypress's sweet flag." He stood almost on her toes and changed the subject. "After our little *tête-à-tête* at Elderson's last night, I spent valuable time with a tow service before I checked the dorm room your pal Angelo calls a studio. Someone made quite a mess of it."

If he was trying to alarm her, he succeeded. She'd

slept very little and even then her grandfather and Angelo popped in and out of her dreams. But she said casually, "My, you do get around. I'd hoped you'd still be hiding under Edna's bed."

"No, but my vantage point did let me hear Edna vehemently accuse Curly Locks of stealing my bronze bowl. Actually, 'that creep' is what she called him."

She ignored his snide comment about Angelo and had already heard from Louis about Edna's rage. "Your bowl? What are you, Italy's watchdog?"

"Via Giulia is my domain. Anyone steals from Rome, I am personally offended."

"Such a good scout."

With his working fingers he pushed aside clothes in the closet, opened her suitcase, felt the drapery, pulled up the mattress.

Only when Mai was sure the gardener had disappeared with the hanging basket did she pick up her portfolio and purse. "Leave a good tip for the maid," she said. When he charged at her, she twisted his swollen fingers. "Stay out of my face, Hunter."

"Dragon Lady." It was a quiet scream, but still a scream. He reached for her arm. She blocked the move.

"Give up," she said. "That bowl is on its way to China."

"And you are Snow White." He cradled his hand.

She turned abruptly and left him standing in the doorway. She hoped he wouldn't notice that the hanging basket was gone. She didn't take time to put the Jaguar's top down, but before she got in, she walked around it to make sure he hadn't punctured the tires.

17

CASABLANCA

Hunter waited until Mai's Jaguar was out of sight before he went back inside her hotel room. He knew she was scheduled to lecture at Coconut Gallery. He'd show up there later. In all probability, she didn't carry the bowl with her anyway. So he took a soda out of the room's small refrigerator and stretched out on her bed.

He really was tired. Jet lag from Rome. Conning info out of Cypress. Casing Elderson's. Broken fingers. Slashed tires. Mai bugged the hell out of him. He clicked on the TV and scrolled to the golden oldie movie channel.

Casablanca. Humphrey Bogart

Okay. Great movie.

He punched the three hotel pillows into a comfortable bulk and laid his head in the nest. Rick's Café. Piano music, "As Time Goes By."

He closed his eyes. The fight with Mai on Elderson's silky bed rustled under him. He wasn't with Rick in Casablanca. He was in Istanbul. With Mai. He sunk into the pillows, trading present for past.

They had both been hunting an Alexandrian scroll. It was stifling. The smell off the Bosporus was foul. The Bosporus stank, but Mai, she smelled of mountain meadows.

He'd been sitting in a seedy bar with a faded green and orange striped awning and a slowly rotating ceiling fan, sipping tonic water. He watched her come in from the sweltering street fanning herself with a bright yellow paper fan from the bazaar. She pulled the bar stool out and sat down next to him, brushing his arm.

"The ice is made with bottled water," he said to her and clinked the cubes around in the glass.

She put the fan down on the bar and shook her damp hair away from her neck. As she brushed a loose stand of hair off her cheek, she turned her body towards him and said to the bartender, "I'll have what the gentleman is drinking."

"Good choice," Hunter said. "Stick with tonic water. Liquor will only make you hotter."

He replayed that meeting in his mind many times. He could not remember how exactly he let slip that the long cardboard tube beside him on the bar contained a valuable scroll he'd purchased for a client. What he did remember was the lilt in her voice and the innocence in her eyes when she said, "An Alexandrian scroll? How fascinating."

And she fanned herself with that cheap paper fan. So naïve, he thought at the time.

He opened his eyes and took another drink of expensive Casa Munras soda. Gently he readjusted the pillows behind his head and closed his eyes again, trying to picture the Istanbul hotel room. The image was sketchy, a grimy window on the third floor, a wooden bed, a thin mattress, one cotton cover. No refrigerator.

However, he visualized every detail of her naked body standing in that nondescript room haloed by the hot sun. And he could still taste the sweat on her neck and smell the spice from the bazaar on her arms and feel her damp stomach as he ran his fingers over her. And there was that hiss. Oh, definitely, he still could hear the hiss of panted air in his ear as she wrapped her legs around him and held him tight. He felt her teeth and tongue. Felt her body. Felt the heat.

That damn heat.

He opened his eyes and stared at the TV. Istanbul was gone, just like Mai was when she made off with the Alexandrian scroll. Gone when he woke then. Gone now.

Goddamn fox.

On the TV, the love of Rick's life got on a plane and took off from Casablanca in the fog.

Hunter got up and straightened his jeans over the tops of his cowboy boots. He was in pursuit of a bowl stolen from his turf and no one was going to get on a plane and fly off with it, not even the love of his life.

18

THE OLD BOWL

James Chang and Mai's grandfather stood in James's bougainvillea covered arbor. James handed the hanging basket to his oldest friend. "A long journey has ended, Daniel."

"I am honored to be in your debt."

James stretched his brown suit coat around his large stomach and fiddled with buttoning it. "Daniel, I'll be all day in court in San Francisco. Find whatever you need here. Stay close to the house. I'm worried. Mai has a way of downplaying danger. She may not have gotten away from Carmel without being recognized." He got into his Lincoln.

Daniel put his hand above the open driver's side window and leaned down. "Do you think Robert Giles-Smyth or that Frank Conti saw either her or Angelo?"

"That's a possibility." He turned the key and started the engine. "Mai will give us details tonight. Until then, don't leave the house."

"Mai cannot be hurt."

"She's clever. Don't fret. Use my library. Find out what you can about the bowl. I'll be home by seven." Before he started up the hill, he stuck his head out the window and called, "One more caution. Hunter knows Mai's connection to me and Interpol."

"Mai's Hunter is here?" Daniel rubbed his hand across his eyes. How had he even thought to involve Mai in this?

"Daniel, you must expect trouble. Even if you just walk on the terraces, keep the bowl locked in the safe. And under no circumstances walk down the hill to the golf course."

Daniel Sung watched the Lincoln disappear and the security gate slowly close. Dangling from his hand, packed in moss, might very well be his ancestor's bowl and his own obligation to the past. The hanging basket was surprisingly light for such a burden. As if he were holding a newborn baby, he felt both excitement and apprehension.

He left the gazania plant and moss with the hanging basket outside. Inside, he brushed off the traces of moss clinging to the bowl and rinsed it gently with a cool stream of water. He patted it dry with a towel. It felt warm in his hands and its blue-green patina surprised him. The color was brighter than he anticipated.

He hurried to the library in the front wing of the house. The room was large and well lit with recessed ceiling lights. He turned the bowl around and around in his hands. It was about five inches deep and eight inches in diameter. He laid it gently on the long walnut library table and searched the corner desk for paper and pencil. Sitting at the table, not at all calm, he drew the bowl, the willow tree with spreading branches, the peacock with long plumes perched on a thick center fork of the tree, the beautiful maiden on a bench. Then he drew it all again as it was upside down and inverted on the inner curve. By pressing another sheet of paper against the scenes and rubbing back and forth on the paper with the Number Two pencil, he also made graphite impressions of them.

The script around the inner rim was not one he knew, not one standardized after 200 BCE, so he had to copy it with careful pencil strokes and a hesitancy he would not have had in his calligraphy practice with ink.

When he finished, his neck and fingers were tense. He made some tea in the kitchen and brought it back into the library. On dark wooden shelves covering every wall were neatly placed volumes, one wall of legal subjects, another of art, a third of history. He pulled out three books on Chinese bronze artifacts.

He loved studying and gradually relaxed. When he used to read to Mai, he never read children's books. Always history. Sitting here, sipping tea, staring at a bowl which he'd learned about so many years ago, he missed Mai. They had grown apart as she grew up. That was the natural course of things. Still, James, working with her case after case, knew her better than he did. He wondered what happened to her childhood dreams. "Grandfather, some day I will fix people just like you do."

After studying the books for some time, he wrote notes on a yellow legal pad. The round shape was typical of the early Western Zhou Dynasty, possibly 1000 BCE. The bird motif would be somewhat later. The calligraphy seemed later still, perhaps Warring States Period of the Eastern Zhou Dynasty, approximately 500 BCE.

He learned that bronze artifacts had been categorized

in the Song dynasty, grouped by use, such as wine vessels or cooking pots.

"I bet this is a *jian*, a water mirror," Daniel said out loud. But his excitement of discovery turned to doubt. If it was a Zhou Dynasty bowl, maybe it was no more than a water mirror. Maybe it was not the temple bowl of his ancestor.

He replaced the books on the shelves. It was too late for doubts. His feet and Mai's were soaking wet in the *I Ching's* river, the river which was dangerous to cross. He'd take this bowl back to China where it belonged as fast as he could.

19

A SCHOLAR'S QUEST

The *putaka putaka* of the Harbor Cruise boat chugging out of the marina at ten a.m. nudged Angelo, but he rolled on the futon to face the wall, too tired to get up. He took momentary notice of the fishy odors from the wharf and tucked the blanket tighter around his head.

In light sleep, he dreamed. He runs in a large house, up steep stairways, down dark corridors, searches frantically for a door or a window. Voices he can't understand shout at him. Water swirls in huge green circles over his head. Ice crunches under tires, metal scrapes against rock. Someone cries.

Angelo woke in a sweat. With his fingertips he wiped his eyes. He took deep breaths until he knew where he was. He hadn't had that dream in more than a year. Contact with Cypress always triggered it.

When he rolled off the futon, his foot landed on the splintered sticks that used to be his easel. On top of that nightmare, his room was a nightmare of its own.

Last night he was too tired to deal with the mess. He had to face it now. He turned the kitchen table back on four legs but before he could pick up the chairs, he watched Helen Frye, Chinese scholar, pain in the butt, prance in front of his window.

"Helen, what can you possibly want?"

She pushed her way into the studio. The look on her face actually made him jump and he had never seen her hands betray such tension as she rubbed them up and down her arms. "I've been waiting all morning for you to come down. Good grief. What happened?"

"Amahl and a night visitor," he said, righting a chair.

"Be serious, Angelo. This is not an opera. Who was here? What were they looking for? Elderson's Chinese bowl?"

Angelo deflected the challenge and glared. "The only thing of value here, darling, is talent, and I was out at the time."

"You know what I mean." Her face was red with anger. "Who did this? Where is the bowl?"

"How in the world would I know?" Of all things, in addition to Edna's, he didn't need another woman's rage.

She jerked a kitchen chair off the large book and eyed the book suspiciously. "If you don't have the Chinese bowl, why are you reading *Secret Knowledge*?" She spit out an accusation. "Brushing up on camera obscuras so you can claim to be an authority? I heard about your radio broadcast. You know it is my theory that Walter's bronze is the earliest representation of a camera obscura. You stole my theory as well as the bowl."

He had a broom in his hand and came very near to sweeping her face with it. In truth, when Walter first showed him the bowl, he had just finished reading Hockney's book. He had an "aha!" moment. He was sure the bowl recorded a scene in a camera obscura. He and Walter had discussed it excitedly. Then, at a private showing of the bowl, Walter asked Helen Frye, big scholar, to confirm that suspicion. Walter never mentioned Angelo. He and Helen planned to announce that theory on TV today. The first to declare a discovery was the first to claim victory. That was the law of the wild in scholarly circles. She was raging because she'd been denied that victory on TV because of his radio promo. Maybe she should rage at Bob-The-Critic who egged him on in the interview.

"Well," Helen said, "are you denying that you checked this book to understand a camera obscura?" Helen thrust *Secret Knowledge* at him. It looked a lot like an asp on its way to Cleopatra's breast.

"Helen. Hockney's theory is impeccable. Let's do lunch another time and discuss yours."

That did it. She grabbed his broom and threw it across the room. With shaking fingers she pinched his arm, hard. "I must know what you know." Her voice trembled. "I want the bowl." She tramped back and forth across the debris. "Can't you see how important it is? I am at my wit's end. I had a press conference scheduled for this afternoon."

She really was a wreck. "I'm sorry, Helen. I can tell you nothing."

"You are a nasty, mean little man." She turned to the door but stopped. Apparently she was not finished.

"By the way," she said. "You might want to read Robert's column in today's *Art Wise Press*." She pulled the paper out of her purse and smacked him with it. Then, in a swirl, she was gone.

After a deep sigh, Angelo said, "Scholars are such bitches."

20

ART WISE

When Mai got to the marina, portfolio in hand, she walked towards Fisherman's Wharf behind a group of preschoolers with bright red name tags, five adults, and a lot of giggles. Lunch lines formed outside restaurants, popcorn popped, fish fried, and ice cream dripped the length of the wharf to Coconut Gallery.

"California in July," she said to Bernie when he waved.

Louis had arranged for her to give a lecture about Chinese brush painting and do a signing of the fancy catalogue which he had printed for her show. It was his idea to auction off a painting and split the proceeds between the gallery and a local *plein-air* painting group whose members were supporters of the gallery.

Before she reached the gallery, Mai detoured to Coconut Café and sat down at a bayside table. She put her portfolio on an empty chair, pushed her sunglasses up, and took a drink of Angelo's beer. "Why are you wearing yesterday's clothes and what's this about your studio?"

"It's a nightmare. Trashed. Edna's doing."

Mai clanked the beer bottle down on the table. "Edna?"

"I think so."

Edna. That came out of the blue. Mai felt her neck stiffen. She thought maybe Hunter had searched the studio himself and laid the blame on an unknown burglar. Still, in light of what Louis had recounted about Edna's behavior last night, she shouldn't have been so surprised.

Angelo said, "I've got two benevolent ladies up there now cleaning. Help me out here." He nudged half a pastrami sandwich towards her.

She had seen him anxious in the past when his projects were almost, but not quite, ready. But that stress was responsible for small lines at the bridge of his nose not deep creases around his eyes. He'd been worrying about more than the project.

He drank some beer. Since neither of them wanted the sandwich, he picked pastrami out of the rye bread and threw it to the gulls. "Edna destroyed my clothes and studio, and Helen came snooping around just now."

"And I saw Louis here last night and Hunter bragged that he checked out your studio."

"It's a bloody revolving door."

"And spinning a lot." She didn't like it.

The waiter brought two more Coronas. "Please, Angelo, do not feed the birds." He shooed the gulls with a napkin.

Angelo pushed his plate to the side. "Yesterday afternoon I went to tell Walter about the camera obscura that I added to the project. Edna may have seen my Jeep. But she wouldn't need that to hate me."

Mai sipped the beer, wondering what to do about Edna. He fed a crust to another gull.

"There's more," he said. He unfolded the *Art Wise Press*. Mai scanned the article.

Last night the peninsula lost two remarkable art treasures. First, the wealthy art collector and popular plastic surgeon Walter Elderson died suddenly at the Coconut Gallery during a showing of Chinese brush paintings by the artist Mai Ling. (You will not want to miss this exhibit. Again Mai superbly demonstrates the depth of ink on paper and silk, calling forth a great reverence for nature and freezing in time the fleeting moments of our lives. See it until the twentieth of next month.) The second treasure, a Chinese Zhou Dynasty artifact recently spotlighted on my radio show, vanished from the Elderson Art Collection last night. We lovers of Walter Elderson and his art join his widow in grieving for both.

Mai let the paper fall to the table. "The insensitive idiot wrote that while he was sitting on the bowl. He announces the theft of the bowl as a cover. Who would think to accuse him after he broke the story? Nice."

Angelo pulled money for the sandwich and beer from his back pocket and folded the bills under the salt shaker.

Mai said, "I'll need to make a condolence call on Edna. I'll convince her to leave you out of this. I hope."

Angelo drained the Corona and stood. "Well, thanks to her, I'm on my way to San Francisco, as if I had nothing else to do but shop for clothes."

They slid the chairs away from the table. "We are invited to James Chang's for dinner. Can you get back by seven?"

"Can we say eight?"

"Yes. Now get away from here." Coming at them from the gallery were Louis and Helen.

"Mai, where have you been?" Helen called, advancing rapidly. "Did you know the Chinese bronze bowl is missing?"

"Hello, Helen," Mai said, stepping aside to give the chair to her. "No. I spent the morning sketching." Telling the truth was clearly out of the question. "Walter's bowl is missing?"

"Not missing. Stolen," Helen said. "Edna is beside herself. Walter dies and we discover the bowl is gone. Since she was in no shape to do so, I told the police. They have to find it."

God she was a loose cannon. Police. Great.

Mai said, "Perhaps you should let Edna deal with the bowl on her own terms."

Louis took Mai's portfolio. "Is this the picture for the auction? You look divine," he said in one breath. "White silk is definitely you. Never mind about the bowl. Your audience is waiting inside. Please, let's go in for the lecture and signing." He gave a brief nod to Angelo. "Shame about your studio."

Mai kept the conversation heading away from Walter and the bowl. "The seabirds this morning were beautiful. We could do a complete show of local birds, Louis. What do you think?" she said, tapping the portfolio and walking with him.

Helen sat down and called to the waiter to bring hot tea with cream. "Why does no one care about the bowl?" she screeched.

21

THE LADY IN GRAY

Angelo headed up the wharf, walking fast, but not fast enough. Bob-The-Critic advanced down the wharf.

"Angelo, I have TV coverage set for Saturday." He lit a cigarette and blew the smoke off to the side, fidgeting more than usual. He patted his coat pockets with quick little thumps. "All this death and missing bowl stuff mustn't interfere. Tell me the drapery will be ready." Angelo had a comment on the tip of his tongue but Bob didn't stop talking. "So sorry about Walter. You must feel awful. Bernie," he called out, "I'll take some of your wonderful chowder."

"Prick," Angelo said, charging full speed ahead.

He continued to Custom House Plaza to check the construction progress. Carpenters had plank flooring laid for the camera obscura on the solid ground of Custom House Plaza. It was an easy construction. All they had to do was follow the hastily drawn blueprints from yesterday and make it look like a cargo crate.

Constructing the frame for the drapery, however, was like putting up a circus tent in strong wind on quicksand. By agreement with the city and state, nothing, including nylon blowing in a gentle breeze, could touch the historic Custom House. And no supporting posts or beams could be sunk in the Plaza. Large platforms had to be built around the Custom House to anchor the scaffolding and secure the guy wires. It was an engineer's worst case scenario.

"Angelo, how on earth did you ever get me roped into this?" the engineer said.

"By telling you the truth. Frankly, you simply are the best. Besides, I gave you a glowing bit in the publicity."

Angelo picked up a hammer and worked for a while. He measured, hammered, hauled lumber. Every now and then his dream flashed in his head and he'd pause, visibly upset. The engineer, probably thinking the labor was too much for him, more than once said, "Angelo, take it easy. You'll pass out."

On the third warning, Angelo gave it up. "You're right. Things look good here. I'd better check the drapery."

He backed his Jeep out of his reserved parking place behind the Maritime Museum and drove to Cannery Row. He double parked beside a truck at the sailmaker's warehouse. Two men were unloading large bolts of gold nylon wrapped in protective plastic from the back of the truck and piling them onto a dolly.

With great relief, Angelo regained momentum.

"You are vindicated," the sailmaker said, standing by the truck's ramp, watching the unloading.

"You never really doubted me and you know it. Are these not beautiful?"

"Beautiful. Symbolizing golden opportunities from the sea, I understand." He patted a bundle as it wheeled by.

"Yes." Angelo, smiling broadly, stopped the dolly and peeled back a corner of the plastic wrap. "You see, golden nylon is just totally indicative of commerce, to quote myself from my radio promo yesterday."

"How did you get so damn modest?" The sailmaker signaled the mover to continue pushing the cloth into the warehouse.

"Long hours of training." Angelo stepped aside so the movers could continue. He shook the sailmaker's hand. "You will make the best drapery and sails ever."

"Me, ten sewing machines, and a cast of thousands." He took his pipe out of his pocket and clenched it, unlit, between his teeth. "By the way, you look like shit."

"Feel that way too."

A loud horn honked. "Hey, idiot, you're blocking the whole friggin' street," a driver yelled at Angelo.

"I must be off," Angelo said to the sailmaker. "Clothing emergency in San Francisco. You are happy?"

"Delirious."

Several hours later, after he finished shopping, with his Jeep full of Armani and Versace, Angelo decided he'd better eat before returning to Monterey. He knew of a sure parking place between dumpsters behind his favorite café on Columbus Avenue.

Turning off Market onto Kearny, he followed a slow bus the whole length of the long flat street. Kearny always made him feel good. The black granite commercial buildings of the Financial District towered on his right, Chinatown and Russian Hill off to his left, the Italian area ahead. Intersecting cultures crowded in on each other like pilgrims in a too small Mayflower.

In the shadows ragged street people wandered. Angelo knew the statistics which insisted that giving money to the homeless solved nothing, but he did it anyway. Stopped at a light, he handed twenty dollars out the window to a barefoot man whose cardboard sign announced, NEED SHOES.

When Angelo came to the EastWest Hotel at the end of Kearny, on an impulse he decided to see the bronze exhibition. So instead of the dumpster parking place, he pulled into the hotel and let a valet park the Jeep.

On the mezzanine in the EastWest Art Gallery he spent half an hour examining the twenty bronze tomb treasures. Like Walter's vessel, they were all intricate, masterful works. There was a tripod ritual vessel with a spout and gold inlay on its two mirror-image dragon handles. On another, men rowed and fish swam around a vase-like pot. Another was an octagonal vessel with yin/yang trigrams on each side.

He particularly admired the octagonal vessel with greenish patina which enhanced the trigrams. Had he seen it before? Perhaps. He knew it was a ritual vessel used for predicting fortunes or misfortunes. It used to be shiny.

For a moment while he looked at it, he felt the warm breeze in the garden that was carved on Walter's bowl. But only for a moment. These bronzes in front of him were dug from tombs. Cold air surrounded him. Death crept into the garden.

He hurried out the main entrance and down the wide stairs to Kearny. After walking at a rapid pace to Columbus Avenue, he slowed down. The fish and chicken odors rounding the corners from Chinese markets on Stockton and Grant were no match for the garlic from the Stinking Rose on Columbus. Fumes from bus exhaust, pizza ovens, and sidewalk coffees eddied around him. Five school girls in blue uniforms, speaking Chinese, broke ranks and hurried past him on both sides. An advertisement for a North Beach porn shop flapped across the sidewalk in front of him.

Angelo allowed Columbus Avenue to fill his head. He crossed to his favorite café at a light. All the inside tables were occupied, so after he got his Greek coffee, lemon rice soup, and baklava, he carried them on a tray to a sidewalk table.

"Do you mind?" the woman said, sitting down next to him in the only other chair in the shade of the awning. His teeth were glued shut with the honey and walnuts of the baklava which he'd eaten first, so he just nodded.

She was twenty-something, maybe thirty, blonde, wearing a gray jacket and burgundy miniskirt. When Angelo saw her minutes ago in the EastWest Art Gallery, he pegged her for a stewardess or a stockbroker.

She set her Greek salad and diet soda almost on the catalogue of tomb treasures which Angelo brought from the bronze exhibit. "Fascinating show," she said, glancing at the catalogue.

Angelo swallowed some coffee from the paper cup to unstick his teeth. "A bit rigid, bronze. I prefer more fluid media," he said.

"Then you probably should head down past Market to Yerba Buena Gardens and the contemporary stuff," she said, spearing a cucumber slice.

"I am contemporary stuff, darling," he said, in no mood for instruction.

"You don't look so contemporary." She eyed him

critically. "More like City Lights Bookstore across the street. Beat, and in need of a clean shirt."

Suddenly he was very tired. "Come to Monterey on Saturday if you want to see real art." He took another sip of coffee.

"I know," she said. "The Custom House Project. You're Angelo." She leaned towards him. "I suspect that more than artistic curiosity brings you to the bronze exhibit."

"Yes. I needed lemon rice soup."

She nodded, put down her fork and turned pages in the catalogue. Then she ate an olive. Then she looked directly into his eyes. "Angelo, I know your camera obscura bronze. Are you selling it to someone at the gallery?"

He swallowed a spoonful of soup. "Firstly, I don't have a camera obscura bronze. And secondly, who are you?"

"Toni Wilson. Among other things, I work in bronze. You would have seen my work if you went south of Market every now and then. Or heard of it if you got out of Monterey more."

"I hear what's important." He twisted in his chair and dumped what was left of his coffee in the trash can behind him.

She squinted a little at him over a spinach leaf and her lips curled slightly.

"You don't look like a metal artist," Angelo said.

"And you don't look like someone who could steal a Chinese bronze bowl." She handed him her plastic knife and his coffee lid to throw away.

He didn't take them. "Your gray jacket projects cool reason. Unfortunately, when you talk it is clear that your gray cells are mush."

She put the knife and lid down. "Word on the street

is that maybe you got hold of Walter Elderson's bowl." She paused. "I think it's likely that your ex, Cypress, told you where to find it."

Now that was totally weird. Not only had she followed him out of the gallery but she was suspicious of him and Cypress. He managed to clear the lump from his throat and say with authority, "The street is never trustworthy." He picked up the catalogue and stood. He noticed a definite hawk-like squint in her eyes, even though her posture remained casual as she handed him a card.

"Take my card," she said, hawk wings spread, swooping low over the field. "You may need me since you have a bowl to sell."

He glanced at the card. Antoinette Wilson, Art Acquisitions, Wilson Imports, Ltd., San Francisco, California. It was his turn to do a bird of prey squint. He tucked the card between two pages of the catalogue. The pleasure of Columbus Avenue left his head. More than a little anxiety replaced it.

22

THE WOMAN IN BLACK

Mai finished the signing at Coconut Gallery and headed to Edna's. Her feet hurt. Summer vacation skipped along the wharf, but she walked slowly back to the Jaguar, out of step with everyone, preoccupied. Could she possibly calm Edna regarding Angelo? Why did Cypress have a paper showing payments from Wilson Imports to Walter Elderson? Did Edna know about the money transfers? Why were things never easy?

On automatic pilot, she drove the Jaguar onto Del Monte Avenue and headed to Pacific Grove. She checked the rear view mirror for Hunter's bike. Several cars back she saw the candy apple red Harley with what must be brand new tires. She shook her head. He would not give up.

As she pulled into Elderson's circular driveway, two cars pulled out. Five others parked along the driveway's curve. Edna probably had visitors all day long, some of them might even have been sorry that Walter was dead. All of them must have been curious about the missing art treasure, thanks to Bob-The-Critic. She set the emergency brake and sat for a minute until she felt ready for Edna.

When she walked towards the door, she heard a bird squawking and followed the sounds to an unfinished garden. A peacock, moving much faster than the man chasing it, circled a pond. When Mai stepped onto the dirt strewn flagstone, the peacock halted on the rim of the pond, lifted its electric blue head, and screeched.

"What's happening here?" Mai asked.

"Good afternoon." The man struggled for breath. "I'm the groundskeeper for the Eldersons." He plopped down on a wooden crate. "Mrs. Elderson wants the bird removed. She says she'll have it shot if it doesn't shut up. I've been trying to catch it for half an hour."

"To no avail, I see. Claws and boots seem to have crossed and re-crossed here many times." Clods of potting soil colored the flagstone a rich brown. Mai picked up a pot of sweet flag. "This looks like something from Carmel Floral Treasures."

"It is. I was helping Ms. de la Mer yesterday with the plants."

The peacock, clearly exhausted, twitched its head, looking with rapid angle changes from Mai to the man. Its shimmering blue neck and black-tipped feather crown danced upside down in the pond water. A good luck peacock which didn't bring luck to Walter. She touched her throat. Her own good luck peacock necklace sat on Angelo's window sill, unless it was one of the things Edna trashed. She'd have to remember to look for it.

Kneeling down, Mai mimicked the bird's cocked head and made cooing noises in the back of her throat, the way she did as a child. The bird came to her. We've met before, it seemed to say, on the roof top, remember? She stroked its neck, calming it, smoothing its feathers. Then she wrapped her arms around it.

"Get off the crate," she said to the groundskeeper. She carried the bird the short distance and eased it into its holding cell. "Don't take it away yet," she said. "Let me check with Mrs. Elderson. If it is all right with her, I'll take it. I'd hate to see its feathers on a hat."

"Thank you." The groundskeeper was as exhausted as the peacock.

She walked up the path lined with rose bushes and onto the marble porch under the stately columns. The ornate door stood ajar. In the living room, a few people in somber colors surrounded Edna who wore another soft Chanel suit, black. All things considered, she looked cool and composed in her classic suit and beautiful setting. But she couldn't have shredded Angelo's clothes and trashed his studio running on cool and composed.

Mai at once realized that her cheerful peonies and seafoam green silk splashed naughtily at the muted colors on everyone else. There was nothing she could do to look less inappropriate.

Shaking hands and greeting several she knew, Mai made her way to Edna. The house was full of funereal flowers, pale yellow roses in crystal vases, faint lavender asters in white baskets, pinkish chrysanthemums tied with gray ribbons. No roadside bouquets from Cypress.

"These flowers are lovely, Edna."

"So many that I've stopped reading the cards. Tea, soda, martini? There's food if you like."

"Some tea, perhaps."

Edna pointed to the drinks and the elaborate spread

of food on a long narrow table in front of the ocean view window. A maid filled a cup for Mai from the silver teapot. Three other guests refilled martinis and admired the view. Clear day. Blue Pacific. A tall gentleman in a dark suit said to the woman in a black dress, "No, Joan, I told you. It wouldn't have mattered."

"But Edna feels just terrible about it," the woman said.

"Look. Even if she had the nitroglycerine, it would not have saved him."

"Shh. Don't talk so loud," the woman said.

Mai stepped in close to the woman who, an hour ago, had purchased Mai's painting of the three hungry birds. "Is there a specific subject I should avoid talking with Edna about?"

"Two subjects, actually. First, the missing art treasure. She turns very red when it's mentioned. Second, nitroglycerine. When Walter had his heart attack last night, Edna tried to find his nitroglycerine. She always carried it for him in her purse when they went out."

"He probably forgot to give it to her," the husband chimed in. "And it couldn't have helped anyway."

Mai glanced at Edna. "I'll talk about other things." She could talk about other things, but she was here to more than mention the art treasure.

Mai took her tea to one of six Chippendale chairs which were arranged in a semicircle in front of the fireplace to accommodate the guests, although everyone except Edna was standing. Mai sat down next to her. "I would like to express my sympathy, Edna. I've always appreciated Walter's and your support of my paintings."

"Purchasing art was Walter's hobby, not mine," Edna

said, clearly dismissing the compliment. It was a comment that didn't mesh with what Mai knew. Edna's father had been an avid collector. In fact, she inherited most of the excellent pieces in this collection. Why was she distancing herself from this collection now? Maybe it was Mai she was distancing from because of her association with Angelo.

"Hobby or serious collecting, either way, you do have a home full of beautiful pieces. That John Singer Sargent over the fireplace is particularly remarkable. It's his early work from Capri, I believe."

Edna nodded so slightly that Mai barely noticed it. What she couldn't help notice was the practiced and lethal stare of the upstairs Medusa which accompanied the nod. Mai acknowledged Edna's reaction. "Did I guess wrong?"

"No. It is a Sargent. Like the one in the sitting room. Not many people know his early work." Edna turned her shoulder slightly away from Mai.

"It's beautiful," Mai said. She would have said something more profound but she was paying attention to a thin thread weaving through her mind, sewing together something about the painting. She forced her attention back to Edna and made a small circle with her tea cup, indicating the chairs. "And Edna, your taste, not Walter's, surely went into the selection of these wonderful Chippendales."

"Do you think so?" Edna said, in a tone still shouting that she wasn't about to be smoothed with compliments and overlook Mai's link to Angelo.

A woman leaned down and kissed Edna's cheek. "Goodbye, dear. Call if you need anything."

Mai sipped the tea, but it was so strong she went back to the buffet and added cream before she went to look closely at the Sargent above the fireplace. The signature looked legitimate.

"Walter was lucky to get this early Sargent," a short man in a dark suit said.

"Do you know this scene?" Mai asked.

"Only since it's been hanging here. An estate in St. Germain put it up for sale and Wilson Imports snatched it up. The Sargent in the other room is a mature work. Having both increases the value of the collection."

"It certainly would do that," Mai said. She worked her way around to the sitting room and studied the Gilded Age portrait hanging above the settee. This portrait was well catalogued, unlike the one in the living room. The thread in her brain ominously stitched away. The Capri painting might be a forgery. Perhaps Wilson Imports and Walter were sewn together tighter than anyone knew.

On her way back to Edna, Mai ran her fingers over the Italian marble bust of a Medici on the mantel. That thread in her brain pulled tight. How many pieces in this collection were black market artifacts or forgeries? It was not unusual for private collectors to have looted or fake treasures. She'd even seen a Dead Sea Scroll fragment in a private home, not to mention gold from the Valley of the Kings like that necklace upstairs in the glass case.

She put her cup down on the cart as the maid gathered martini glasses from the coffee table. The last sympathizer, a woman in navy blue, kissed Edna on the cheek. "Stop worrying. Call me if you need anything, anything at all."

Mai was alone with Edna. She sat down next to her.

To ease into the touchy subject of Angelo, Mai, actually feeling real sympathy, asked, "What are you worried about?"

Edna swallowed the last of her martini. "I usually carry Walter's nitroglycerine, but it wasn't in my purse." She'd been drinking too much, spoke too slowly. She walked to the mantel and turned the marble head, adjusting something more than the bust of a Medici. With candor, as if in church confession, she said quietly, "Most of the time, I hated Walter. But I wish I'd had his pills when he needed them."

Edna took her fury out on Angelo as she probably had on countless others that Walter had been involved with. Now she blamed herself for Walter's death. Did she also take the blame for Walter's indiscretions? Stoic Chanel suits notwithstanding, Edna's life with Walter must have been one terrifying rollercoaster ride of betrayal and reconciliation.

Mai did not envy the hard tasks Edna had ahead of her, sorting out dozens of contradictory feelings. Still, she had to convince Edna not to take aim again at Angelo and convince her that he did not have the bowl. She decided to be blunt, attack from the front.

"Well, Edna, at least now there is no need for Angelo to trouble your life. You trashed his studio last night. That ought to be revenge enough."

The grieving widow morphed instantly into the humiliated and furious wife. She almost knocked the Medici off the mantel. "How dare you mention that conniving creep. He used Walter. He stole his Chinese bronze bowl."

Mai faced her. "Angelo is a complex person who had an unfortunate affair with Walter. But I know him. He did not steal the Chinese bowl from Walter."

"He's about as complex as a slimy worm. Don't defend him in this house. Get out."

Mai didn't budge. "Why do you think it was Angelo who stole the bowl?"

"Because he was here yesterday afternoon. I saw him."

Great. What Angelo feared was right. She had seen his Jeep parked under the eugenia hedge yesterday afternoon. "You saw him here?"

"His Jeep drove by me when I came home from the hair salon."

With a quick breath of relief, Mai softened her tone. "Edna, you are an intelligent woman. Think. Angelo goes to Cannery Row and Pacific Grove all the time. That doesn't prove anything."

"I'll let the police sort it out." The challenge in her voice was unmistakable. A strand of her perfect hair fell from the ash blonde French twist.

Mai did not let the challenge go. She did not raise her voice. She lowered it. And took a step towards Edna. "You are in a firestorm, Edna, and that Chanel suit will not protect you. That bowl was black market and I think you know it. Shall the police sort out the rightful owner?"

Edna set her jaw tight. "Leave me alone." With sharp twisting steps she reached the long table and filled a martini glass with gin.

Mai followed and moved the bottle to one side. "Do you really want the police to sort things out and splash Walter's affair with Angelo all over the front page of every peninsula paper? Or," Mai pushed into very secret territory, "examine this art collection? How many pieces here have no provenance? Are looted or forged? An artist like

Angelo probably would benefit from a scandal. A collector never does." She paused for effect. "Will you?"

Edna fussed with the strand of hair which dangled on her neck. She stared out the window. Her stiff posture weakened. "This is hell."

It must have taken enormous energy for Edna to live with Walter, be humiliated by his affairs, have her art collection compromised. She had created a façade to cope with both. Mai had just hammered it down. Edna didn't look so good.

Mai wanted to apologize for hurting her and relieve some of the pressure on her. She wasn't sure how. But Edna had already confessed a major secret to her, that she hated Walter. Confessing to a stranger was often easier than confiding in a friend. Mai could be an appropriate stranger. Maybe if she calmly brought another secret into the open, Edna could cope with it rather than be crushed by it.

Mai guessed at the meaning of the payments from Wilson Imports and the suspect art. "You and Walter didn't really own the bronze bowl, did you? It was a sort of loan from Wilson Imports, like this Sargent portrait and Medici bust."

Edna took off her jacket and sat down on the red velvet sofa. Fatigue, sorrow, anger, gin, all seemed to press her down. She rested her head on the red velvet and closed her eyes. "Walter was supposed to keep the bowl, like the other pieces, to give it a respectable provenance so Toni Wilson could sell it at a high price from a known collection. She paid him a share of those sales. But the manager of the EastWest Art Gallery wanted to buy it immediately. Christie's was going to appraise it. I told Walter that would cause trouble." She shook her head back and forth on the velvet. "I don't know. I guess someone else could have stolen it."

Edna opened her eyes, raised her head, straightened her back, and replaced pieces of her façade by regaining perfect posture. "Do you always bring this much joy with you?"

Mai sat at eye level with her. "Don't worry, Edna. I have no intention of telling anyone your secrets. Let Angelo be the past. Let the bowl be the past. You are a strong woman. You can recover from Walter's mistakes."

Edna nodded, whether in agreement or resignation Mai couldn't tell.

On her way out, Mai walked by the long table of food, half a sliced ham, melted brie, crackers, rolls, a few strawberries dipped in chocolate, an uncut apple pie, all left by the ocean view window. The remains of the day. Remains. Scraps. Death. Sad times in this gorgeous house.

Outside, pink blossoms swayed in a slight wind. "Help," the peacock cried weakly from the crate.

"I didn't ask, but since Mrs. Elderson wants it gone, I'll take the peacock," Mai said to the groundskeeper who was now smoothing soil with a rake around the planted sweet flag. He carried the crate to the Jaguar but couldn't fit it in the door.

"Forget the crate," Mai said. "I'll take it *alfresco*."

Mai lifted the bird out and maneuvered it onto the passenger seat, tucking its tail between the bucket seats. Its crest fluttered just above the headrest.

Mai got in. "Where to?" she asked the peacock. "I saved you from the hatter so wherever we go, no crying."

With the gearshift under a heap of feathers, shifting

was a challenge but Mai finally got into first and pulled slowly out of the driveway. In her rear view mirror she saw the groundskeeper leaning on his rake, laughing. On Ocean View Boulevard, in her rear view mirror, she saw Frank Conti's car, dented front and all, pull away from the curb into the lane behind her.

He had linked her to Robert's Carmel cottage.

And even worse, Conti's car was followed by a candy apple red Harley.

Her pulse thumped in her neck. Two against one, unless the peacock could fight.

23

MEMORIES

Angelo's Jeep was not a comfortable touring car and the drive back to Monterey piled more fatigue on top of his worry. His projects usually were finished only at the last minute. But with this one, he really was cutting it close. The drapery required time. He wasn't sure the sailmaker and his workers could sew fast enough. And he usually wasn't in the sights of an irate woman. And, God, who was this lady in gray who knew that Cypress had the bowl?

Cypress. He could go months without worrying about her, their lives separated by the past.

Traffic stacked up on the narrow road between Salinas and Monterey. The slow drive gave him time to think. He couldn't shake Cypress from his head.

He remembered the afternoon they'd met, the overcast sky with its low clouds touching the choppy sea. He had climbed aboard a yacht with half a dozen others to scatter the ashes of a close friend. Cypress carried the urn. She was the only one on the boat that he didn't know.

The yacht maneuvered out of the marina under power but the sail snapped taut and the boat lurched in the waves beyond the shelter of the bay.

He sat next to Cypress out of the way of the boom, watching the bow cut a white path through rough water. Three miles out in open sea gentler waters accepted the cremated remains of their mutual friend. Cypress said that here the Lord of the Sea sat on a grand throne surrounded by sea horses waiting to welcome their friend. She didn't seem unhappy on that sad occasion. That was seven years ago when they were both twenty-one.

Traffic stopped. A flagman waved a red stop sign. After Angelo turned the engine off, he put his elbow on the window frame and leaned his head out. He couldn't see beyond the curve of the road and the line of cars.

When he and Cypress were first married, they lived with her grandmother in a 1930 cottage in Carmel. Her grandmother had lived her whole life on the rugged coast. She loved the wildness of it and the comfort of the cocooning fog. She gave Cypress the nickname, de la mer, because, she said, Cypress was as wild as the Big Sur surf.

Cypress and her grandmother spent hours every day painting on the cliffs. She taught Cypress to sketch so that a sketch became more than the bare bones of a picture. They would put little pots of watercolors on the kitchen table and her grandmother would say "make the color of morning glories, make the color of the Mission's stucco, make the color of evening light."

Her grandmother had been a remarkable artist. He still had a few of her paintings, the ones he and Cypress didn't sell when she died.

The Jeep was confining. Angelo stepped out onto the

pavement and walked ahead a little to see what the delay was. He couldn't see the problem. Other drivers were also out pacing. He sat back on the front seat but dangled his legs out the door, one foot on the running board. Across the road oak trees rustled and dry grasses blew in the breeze.

When Cypress made coffee in the morning, he would sit at the tiny kitchen table. He loved those mornings. The minute the coffee maker started to gurgle, Cypress would beat time with a spoon and sway her hips.

When Cypress painted, she sang like the coffee pot. Crazy notes that he'd never heard before, melodies she made up one day and could never duplicate the next. She said the music helped her brush find its way around the paper. And her colors sang, too. Opera reds, choir yellows, bluegrass greens. She painted little things, a pebble, a button, a pine needle covered with dew, a drop of milk falling in a cup, the stray cat's nose.

They tacked those pictures on every wall.

Cypress threw them away when their baby died. She blamed herself for the car crash. But it was the ice. A car rounded the curve in her lane going too fast. She swerved. The tires skidded. She was hit hard from the side, pushed into the rocks on the road cut. She couldn't get the baby out before the fire started. She wanted to be the one who died. She tried to paint again, but she never sang or danced. She finished just one painting, the lone cypress tree with its twisted limbs and raging sea foam. It hung in her office at Carmel Floral Treasures. The tree wasn't beautiful to her, just angry, unable to grow in a natural way, distorted by the wind, changed forever by that isolated spot on the cliff. He lost both the baby and Cypress in that accident five years ago.

Cars followed a pilot car going the opposite direction in the lane next to him. Whatever had the traffic backed up had cleared. Angelo swung his legs inside the Jeep and started the engine.

The flagman waved him on. He continued his journey without Cypress.

And she without him.

24

THE MALL

After leaving Edna's, Mai drove to Monterey in late afternoon traffic which was triple the usual volume. Every car on the peninsula jammed into Monterey for Angelo's weekend extravaganza. No way she could lose Conti or Hunter in stop-and-go traffic and she wasn't about to lead them to her hotel room or on a tour of the peninsula.

"Hang on," she said to the peacock which had its beak out the slightly lowered passenger window. On a red light, she swerved into the Del Monte Shopping Mall. She watched Conti in her side mirror run the same red light in front of the oncoming traffic and turn behind her.

When she got into the parking area, she wondered if this was such a hot idea. There were cars cruising for parking places and pickup trucks bullying into COMPACT ONLY spaces. She wouldn't look for minutes for a parking place with Conti on her tail. She wanted to get rid of him. So she parked in a blue striped handicapped space and left both windows halfway open for the peacock. Then she limped towards the center of the mall and turned into a bookstore to hide.

In the center aisle of the bookstore, she waited by the New Paperbacks table to see if Conti tracked her, turning over books with eye catching covers to read the back blurbs. Several customers came in but only one stopped downstream of her to look at gift books, Frank Conti.

Damn. He was faster than she thought he would be. She moved on to New Nonfiction, walked through the rows of Health and Fitness, then turned to Mystery and stopped against the wall at the end of a row where she couldn't be seen except by someone coming directly towards her.

She pulled Arturo Pérez-Reverte off the shelf and read the title page of *The Fencing Master.* She turned the page, biding her time, and finished three sentences of the first paragraph when Frank Conti rounded the corner.

He wore a light linen suit. It was hard to imagine that he actually lifted treasures from digs or smuggled them across the sea with those manicured fingernails and two hundred dollar haircut. Last night, though, soaked by Bob-The-Critic's garden hose, he didn't look so classy.

Tired of the cat-and-mouse game, more precisely, tired of being the mouse, she carried Arturo Pérez-Reverte in her hand and headed towards Conti along the Mystery novels. She stopped, reached up, and pulled Anne Perry off the shelf and plopped her on top of Arturo, added Elizabeth George to the stack nestled in her arms, and finally Walter Mosely. Then she deliberately plowed into Frank Conti. Mosely and George slid off her pile. Frank caught the two books.

"Oh. Hello," Mai said, innocently. "I didn't see you

standing there. Are you and Toni still in town?" She adjusted the two books in her arm. "I love good mysteries." Then she employed the stare she had learned from Edna and Medusa. "If you want to get a latte with me next door, we could solve the mystery of why you are following me."

Her attack worked. He slapped the two books back on her stack hard enough to jar her arm downward. "You took something of mine last night," he said.

"You are mistaken."

"I don't think so. It was definitely you throwing the hose around Robert's house last night."

"I'm sure you're wrong," she said. "There was quite a lot going on last night with Walter Elderson's death, but none of it involved me, you, and a hose." She pushed his body away from her with Arturo Pérez-Reverte. At the cashier she bought the books. At the exit door Frank bumped her with his shoulder.

Mai clutched the plastic bag with the four books and stepped away. Frank patted his breast pocket and what Mai figured was his shoulder holster, probably holding a gun with an elegant pearl handle. She said, "I'm not much for threats or melodrama." With a grand swooping arc, she slung the plastic bag over her shoulder.

At the coffee shop across from the bookstore she bought a latte and watched to see if he followed. He did. He was a short distance behind her when she reached her car.

"You know you're being followed?" Hunter asked, perched sidesaddle on his bike, one boot on the footrest, one on the blue stripe of the Keep Clear handicapped ramp next to Mai's car. He rested his splinted fingers on the handlebars.

"Can't a girl have a latte without being harassed?" She held the coffee and books in one hand and with the other fished for her car keys in the red dragon purse.

"I waited for you at Elderson's," Hunter said. "Expressions of sympathy must have been hard on your face. I mean, you had to keep it straight while saying 'so sorry your husband died' without mentioning that you snitched his very valuable Chinese bowl. No wonder your visit with Edna took so long."

"Did you have a timer going?"

A couple of old ladies passed the Jaguar. "Dears," one called, "I think that animal needs help."

Mai thrust the bag of books and her latte cup into Hunter's arms and hurried to the Jaguar to calm the peacock. The interior of the car looked like a huge fan from a strip tease act, bright blue-green feathers pressed window to window. Two sharp claws gripped the seats on either side of the gearshift and it pecked, pecked, pecked with rapid fire head jolts at its own image in the rear view mirror.

"Take it easy," Mai said. She pushed its chest backward until it backed up and compressed itself into the very small space behind the two seats. Mai angled the mirror down so that it couldn't see a reflection.

"What's with the peacock?" Hunter asked, peering in the open door. "Ouch!" He jerked his arm. "The damn thing pecked me."

"Well, move back," Mai said. She closed the door.

"Take these." He unloaded the books and latte onto the Jaguar's hood and rubbed the blood off his upper arm. "I suppose that bird is a registered art treasure."

"My new best friend. Birds are nicer than some people."

"That one's not." He sat down on his Harley. "By the

way, while I was waiting for you to come out of Elderson's I noticed that tan car with the dented hood parked by the curb until you drove out of the driveway. Then it followed you. He's not too subtle."

"Who?"

Hunter tilted his head sideways. "There, end of the row, tan car, slashed tires."

"You are so low tech. Slashing tires. Is that the best you can do?" The peacock squawked.

"I was reminded of that spiffy technique for disabling a vehicle just last night."

"Maybe you should be more careful where you park."

He stood. "I want to know who this guy is. If he's following you because you have the bowl, he's in my way."

"I'm going home." She jingled her keys.

A mall security car pulled in on the other side of the Jaguar. A uniformed officer got out and walked around. "I don't see a handicapped plate on this car, Miss."

"Bit of a handicap carting that peacock around," Hunter said.

The peacock sat in the passenger's seat again, bobbing its head out the window. Mai pushed its head inside, opened the door, brushed untamed feathers out of her face and managed to reach into the glove compartment while holding the peacock's chest out of the way with one hand. She pulled one of her standard tools from the glove compartment, a laminated handicapped card. "I'm sorry, officer. I forgot to hang this on the mirror."

The guard turned to Hunter. "And you, sir? Have a handicap as well?"

Hunter held up his splinted fingers.

"Sorry. Not exactly disabling. I need to see a permit.

'Fraid I'll have to write you up."

Hunter glared at Mai. "You make my life so difficult."

Mai limped her way around to the driver's side and grabbed the coffee cup and books off her hood.

"Look officer," Hunter explained, "I'm just waiting for a friend who went to call a tow truck. All his tires are slashed. Down that row." He brandished his injured hand with a flourish of his wrist.

"I'll check that out for you," the officer said, and stuck the ticket between Hunter's splinted fingers.

Mai backed slowly out of the space. Conti glared at her from behind Hunter. Hunter shot daggers at her. She smiled.

25

CASA DE CHANG

Mai stopped by the marina to pick up Angelo for dinner.

Earlier, while the peacock snooped around her Casa Munras room, she changed from her silk clothes to a peach cotton blouse and white slacks. She considered canceling dinner, not wanting to lead either Hunter or Conti to Pebble Beach and her grandfather. But Conti was out of commission thanks to Hunter, and Hunter would now be following Conti. And both her boss and her grandfather wanted to meet Angelo to thank him for his help in retrieving the bowl.

Angelo and Mai pushed most of the peacock into the tiny back space behind the seats so Angelo could get in. Tail feathers stuck up here and there. Angelo wore new tan flannel trousers, Ferragamo loafers, no socks, and an ivory shirt with billowing pleated sleeves gathered at the wrists by wide cuffs held closed with three buttons.

"This must be what Hamlet is wearing this season," Mai said, spreading the gorgeous pleats even farther apart with her fingers.

"Probably in Act V. My studio is a trash heap again."

"What?" Mai pushed the peacock's head out of her way so she could see Angelo. "Say that again. Someone searched your studio a second time?"

"Apparently. On Columbus Avenue this afternoon, a lady in gray told me word on the street was that I had the bowl and got it from Cypress."

"What lady in gray?"

"Some lady in a gray jacket. Toni something."

"Toni Wilson? How were you talking to her?" Mai had yet to pull into the traffic. Her foot stuck firmly to the brake pedal.

"She was in the EastWest Art Gallery when I looked at the bronzes. She must have followed me."

"That's not good. Toni plays her game on the black squares not the white. She doesn't return artifacts. She brokers them. Walter's bowl came to her through Conti."

"Well, no one found it today. And waiting for the drapery to be ready is killing me." He slumped. "Let's go eat."

Mai pulled onto Del Monte Avenue thinking they might not make it to "curtain going up" for *Hamlet*, let alone Act V since neither she nor Angelo was invisible to Edna, or Conti, or Hunter, and now, Toni.

"Are you all right?" Angelo asked, leaning forward to peer around the peacock's head at Mai. "You stopped talking."

She didn't share her worry. He'd been through enough. They both needed a change in subject. "Thank God for new clothes." She stroked the peacock's neck and glanced around it. "You look great."

When they arrived at the gate of 17-Mile Drive, the

guard waved the Jaguar on without even glancing at the crested head and bulk of feathers. Mai wound the car around cypress and pine trees into the hills above Pebble Beach and through the gate onto the grounds of one of the oldest homes in this dramatic area, Casa de Chang the local wags tagged it now, tongue-in-cheek, a sideways comment on Chinese amid the Spanish.

Trees lined the long entry road down the slope to the rock and wooden beam house. Below it, the top of the sun dipped its last rays into the ocean sending yellow and orange flashes through the branches.

James and Mai's grandfather walked through the bougainvillea arbor as Angelo lifted the peacock out and let it down on the wild hillside. It did not move.

James opened Mai's door. She usually saw him when he wore a business suit so his white turtleneck sweater and brown slacks surprised her. He seemed just as round and just as imposing.

"We have the bowl in the safe," he said. Then, staring at the peacock, he added, "Mai, I am used to you showing up with beautiful objects. Usually, however, they do not breathe."

Mai laughed. "This gorgeous one I saved from the hatter today and this one is my very dear friend, Angelo, breathing well, I am relieved to say, after a trying day and also looking incredible."

Mai's grandfather shook Angelo's hand. "I am happy to meet you at last, Angelo. Mai speaks highly of you. Forgive my appearance. Mai dropped me here last night with only a few clothes. I'm afraid this plain shirt is no match for either peacock or artist."

Her boss extended his hand. "I'm James."

"Mai speaks highly of you both," Angelo said, shaking hands.

"The peacock is worn out," Mai said.

"Let's put it somewhere safe," her grandfather said, immediately in good rapport with the frazzled bird. He gathered it into his arms.

They walked along the cobblestone path to the open front door, roughhewn, weathered oak boards bound together by black metal. "Great door," Angelo said.

The house was built in 1920 by a devotee of Frank Lloyd Wright and it hovered on the steeply terraced hillside, a single story of horizontal wooden beams and vertical supports of stone.

Mai watched her grandfather carry the peacock through the long living room and out the glass door in a wall of floor-to-ceiling windows. He let it down on the deck. The bird, so high above the water and in the midst of so many branches, immediately hopped onto the wooden arm of a deck chair and roosted.

"Magnificent house," Angelo said. The living area was an expanse of mahogany flooring, waxed and reflective. The dark planks extended beyond the west wall of windows to form the deck which ran the width of the house. Under the cantilevered deck the hillside dropped away sharply.

The interior walls of the house were stark white. Not one painting, tapestry, or object hung on them. Instead, the room was dominated by the fireplace, a sculpture of brick and granite, red and gray chunks of uneven thicknesses which were interrupted midway to the ceiling by a polished red oak mantel.

On a table of ebony in front of the fireplace, gardenias floated in a ceramic bowl, infusing the room with a sweet scent. Around the table, a small sofa and two chairs formed a sitting area, their backs shiny vertical slats of cherry wood, their cushions soft brown leather. A white wool rug, woven with knotted yarns, fit exactly under the furniture.

As they walked through the room, they passed six irregularly spaced, small windows on the wall opposite the fireplace. Six, a yin number. They framed sections of the outside pines whose shadows cast moving designs on the wall.

"Come look here," Mai said from the west wall which was actually nine separate windows framed in blonde oak. Mai liked that. Nine. A potent yang number. The power of light. "In the bright sun, the bevels at the top of each window split the light into rainbows," she said. "The whole room dances in color."

"This is wonderful space." Angelo said.

"I'm glad you like it," James said. "Mai tells me you are a difficult critic to please."

Mai's grandfather came in from the deck. "I don't think the peacock will move."

"Good," James said. "I brought sourdough bread from the city. Let's make dinner." He folded back a section of an ornate ivory and jade screen which separated the dining area from the kitchen. In the kitchen he pulled a knife from a drawer and handed it to Angelo. "I think you will find onions and peppers in the refrigerator, Angelo. Mai, garlic and oil in that cabinet." He grabbed a corkscrew from another drawer and a bottle of cabernet from the wine rack.

"James can make Chinese dumplings look like ravioli

but marinara sauce is out of his league," Mai's grandfather said, lifting two melons from a bowl on the countertop in front of more windows.

"You slice that melon for an antipasto, Daniel," James said. "Pretend you are in surgery."

"He is good with melons," Mai added. She got out the garlic and olive oil and put them on the center work island's cutting board.

"I think it is racial profiling to ask me to make the marinara sauce," Angelo said, his hands full of tomatoes from a bowl on the counter.

"What? White guy from Fresno?" Mai said, taking a sauce pan from the hanging rack above the island. "The only Italian you know is *ciao*."

She was glad to hear Angelo laugh. She poured oil in the pan, lit the burner under it, and smashed four garlic cloves with the blade of a broad knife by hitting it with the heel of her hand.

"This is the most fun I've had all summer," her grandfather said as he arranged melon slices in a star pattern on a white plate.

"And probably the best food, since you've been cooking for yourself," James said.

"Wine and Italian food," Angelo said, tossing his diced tomatoes and peppers into Mai's warming olive oil. "What more could we need?"

"Art," they said in unison and laughed.

The sauce simmered, cabernet, melon, and bread disappeared, and finally ravioli hit the boiling water. James handed out square green dishes and chopsticks for them to carry to the cherry wood dining table and opened another bottle of wine.

"I am absolutely certain that I have never eaten ravioli with chopsticks," Angelo said.

"Your culinary education is in need of expansion," Mai's grandfather said. "Pay attention." He picked up one precisely crimped cheese ravioli with his chopsticks and waited for Angelo to do the same.

"If I can drape a historic monument with thousands of yards of nylon, this will be a piece of cake." He picked up a ravioli but his chopsticks slipped and the ravioli skidded across his plate.

"Hold tighter," James said.

"Words to live by," Mai said, and popped a whole ravioli into her mouth.

Later, they carried bowls of vanilla gelato and fresh strawberries onto the deck. The moist evening breeze brushed the deck with the fragrance of nearby cypress and pine and carried from farther down the scents of newly mown grass from the golf course.

Instead of sitting at the small table in the corner of the deck, they pulled four deck chairs into a little campfire grouping. Mai put her gelato on the arm of the chair facing the hillside and stood at the railing surveying the land below and the security gate above.

When she turned back, her grandfather said, "I am afraid, Angelo, you are caught up in my destiny."

"That is an understatement," James said, scraping the wooden legs on the deck as he pulled the chair closer, tightening the circle.

Mai brought them up to date. "Last night Louis came looking for Angelo, Edna ransacked his studio, and Helen showed up on his doorstep this morning." She picked up her gelato and sat down. "This afternoon I had run-ins with Edna, Frank Conti, and Hunter." She tried to sound casual. "Apparently Conti recognized me last night."

James peered over his glasses at her and with that one look set her heart racing. Conti was trouble, evidently more than she wanted to acknowledge.

"Where?" her grandfather asked, in his quiet, worried tone.

Mai recounted the bookstore conversation.

Angelo put his spoon in his empty bowl. "And Toni Wilson thinks I have the bowl. Someone searched my studio again this afternoon."

Mai's grandfather wiped his glasses with a napkin as he stood and paced the length of the deck and back. "Angelo, Mai, both on radar screens. And here we sit, together, in your house, James. That makes you a target too. I don't like it."

"My house is safe," James said. His voice was clinical, calm. "Don't worry." He stepped to the doorway. "Mai, before you get too comfortable, help me with espresso."

Mai hesitated, one foot inside the house, one still on the deck. Her grandfather, seemingly reassured about the safety of the house, sat down and said, "The Chinese bronze bowl is a unique treasure but not an auspicious one. I am sorry, Angelo."

Angelo leaned back in his chair and crossed his arms behind his head, staring up at the first stars of the evening. "It's not the bowl. It's my relationship with Cypress and Walter that makes me a suspect. That's nobody fault but mine."

"I appreciate your saying that. I understand now why Mai is so fond of you. However, I feel that I owe you a rather long explanation."

"Brief or long, after the day I've had, I am happy to listen." Angelo straightened his arms and sat focused on Mai's grandfather.

Mai was not sure she wanted Angelo to know the whole story of the bowl.

"My wife was born in Locke," her grandfather said. "So was I. Our parents emigrated from the Zhongshan District in China. We all worked the pear orchards in Locke. It's a ghost town now, sadly. I remember crowds, school games, noise, smoke, sore muscles."

Her grandfather's voice was strong and reassuring. If he wanted Angelo to know about his life and the bowl, that was fine. Only when she reached this conclusion did she follow James into the kitchen.

In the kitchen James tamped coffee into the measured press and inserted it in the espresso machine. "The combination to the safe is still the same, just in case you need the bowl and I'm not here."

Mai took out the small espresso cups from the cabinet. "Edna Elderson was hell-bent on talking to the police but I think I convinced her otherwise." The espresso steam hissed. "And she admitted in confidence several things which I can't tell you. But Walter knew that the bowl was looted."

James stopped scooping coffee. "Walter and Toni. A convergence of evil," he said.

He talked like that when connections caused him serious concern. He poured the first shot of coffee into an insulated carafe.

They were silent as Mai arranged the cups on a bamboo tray. The espresso machine hissed again. He filled the carafe.

"Mai, one other connection. We think Frank Conti is responsible for the death of a trader in Rome at the site where the sorcerer's naked lady effigy and the bowl were discovered."

"I'll be careful."

"Everyone needs to be more than careful. In fact, you and Daniel need to take the bowl and leave as soon as possible. I'll arrange a flight to China." He picked up the tray and carried it out.

Mai's grandfather was still narrating. "I try to return to Locke as often as I can to write and tend melons."

"I grew up in Fresno," Angelo said. "I'm an only child. My father is a chemist, my mother a civil engineer. I am a misfit in their world. No Locke of my own."

Angelo and her grandfather had certainly established an easy exchange of personal details. While James held the tray, Mai poured hot coffee and handed each a cup. She sat down and tucked her legs up on the chair pad.

Her grandfather began again. "Our families moved from Locke to San Francisco. We married and our beautiful daughter, Lily, was born. My wife died three years later." He paused, as if lost in that memory.

The peacock on the far chair raised its head and jumped down, the lumbering weight of its tail dragging the chair's cushion halfway to the deck.

Mai sat up. "Something is moving among the cypress on the bottom terrace."

"Where?" her grandfather asked, stretching up to see over the railing.

"We have deer," James said, with no alarm in his voice. "They move about down there at night. I'll go check."

Mai readjusted her legs underneath her. Her grandfather took a sip of espresso. The peacock nested again, this time on the pad of a deck chair nearest the edge. Mai's grandfather slowly replaced the cup on the saucer. It was half a minute before he spoke again.

"I have Mai's picture here."

"Grandfather," Mai said in horror. "You don't still carry that schmaltzy photo, do you?"

"Of course." He pulled out his wallet and handed it to Angelo. Angelo squinted at the photo of a young girl holding a cupcake with five candles.

Her grandfather took back the wallet. "My daughter and son-in-law were killed in a traffic accident."

A breeze rubbed pine needles together and the surf murmured far below. Quietly, simply, Angelo said, "I hear a car crash like that myself." He rubbed his forehead with both hands. Mai touched his arm. Her grandfather studied him.

James came back onto the deck. "Nothing down there. All clear."

"Well," her grandfather said, "I think it is remarkable that the bronze bowl which brought us together tonight had a peacock cast on it more than two thousand years ago, and now we have this peacock in this garden."

"An amazing connection," Angelo said. He sat up straight and looked first at Mai's grandfather, then Mai, and turned to stare at James. "It feels so strange to be linked to each of you and to an ancient world."

"Okay," Mai said, pulling her legs out from under her. "This is getting spooky. If we keep it up we will soon be plotting our intersecting destinies in the stars beginning with the heavens of 500 BCE."

"We could," James said with clear delight and a hand

clap. "I have star charts."

"He does, you know," her grandfather said, and patted Angelo's shoulder.

"Let's go in," James said. "I have work to do. Court tomorrow. Daniel, why don't you make a small fire. You three could use its comfort."

26

THE ORACLE BOWL

Inside, Mai turned on the recessed lighting in the ceiling. Her grandfather gathered some twigs and one log from a wooden box and placed them in the fireplace.

After leaning over to smell the gardenias on the coffee table, Angelo sank into the soft leather chair. Mai struck a long match, watched the twigs flame and the pine log begin to catch fire, then sat in the chair opposite Angelo.

"I studied the bowl this morning," her grandfather said. "I think it is a *jian*."

"I've studied it at Walter's," Angelo said, "but he never called it a *jian*."

"A water mirror," Mai said. "A little reflecting basin. I've not even had a chance to look carefully at it."

"I'll get it," her grandfather said. He brought the *jian* from the safe and with two hands offered it to Mai. She stared at it as if, after a long search, she'd found it in a secret treasure room.

"Let's try it," Angelo said.

"What do you mean?" Mai's grandfather asked.

"Well, it is a reflecting bowl," Angelo said. "Let's look in it."

"You know," Mai's grandfather said, "I sketched it, measured it, worried about it, but I never thought to use it."

"I'll fill it," Mai said. She carried the bowl to the kitchen and when she returned, set it down on the low table in front of Angelo and moved the gardenias out of the way. After brushing a little water off her slacks, she sat on the white rug close to the table.

From his chair, Angelo leaned over the bowl.

"What do you see?" Mai asked.

"Only the upside down garden."

"Focus on the surface of the water, not the side of the bowl," Mai's grandfather suggested.

Angelo slid off the chair and knelt on the white rug opposite Mai. He looked directly down. "Now I see the reflection of the writing along the rim and the lights in the ceiling."

"Find yourself," Mai said. Her grandfather sat down on the hearth and crossed his legs.

Angelo looked for several more seconds.

"Oh, okay, now, there's my face." He stared into the bowl.

"What does your face tell you?" Mai asked.

Angelo did not take his eyes off his reflection. He seemed to form thoughts as slowly as his face had formed in the water. At last he spoke. "Gentle loves too soon are lost. Willows wither and peacocks cry. Cloudless skies turn quickly gray, and woman's tears like raindrops fall."

Mai had never heard Angelo speak of loss with such a melancholy voice. She suspected that Cypress flooded his memory. The bowl allowed him to express a tender connection with his past. "That was beautiful," she said. Her grandfather nodded.

Angelo smiled at both of them and pushed the bowl across the table to Mai. "Your turn."

Just as her fingers touched the bowl, she felt a sharp pain and heard a snap. She jerked. "Static electricity. That's a surprise."

"Careful," her grandfather said.

Mai ran her fingers slowly over the outer curve of the bowl. On her fingertips, the delicate indentations and swellings in the bronze felt like soft willow leaves, and the tiny features of the woman's face seemed magnified as if Mai were carefully examining her own features. She felt a silken gown, cool as jade, a body lotus warm. What lover would not come to this garden, pass the day beneath this willow, wrapped in jade, entwined in flowers?

Looking into the water, she scrolled backwards in time, turning centuries like pages in her calendar, until she felt face to face with the woman under the willow. She saw a latticed window, a palace window, in the wall behind the woman. Who was she? Consort of a king? Courtesan from the pleasure quarters? An artist's ideal woman? Whoever she was, she sat alone.

Mai tipped her head slightly to the side. "I hear the woman singing. I know the melody." With her fingers clasped around the bowl and her eyes closed, Mai sang.

Green spring's soft rain comes round.
A willow's new leaves shade a garden bench.
High in the tree a peacock roosts,
Beneath, a maiden sings ten thousand songs.
Ten thousand flowers bud,
Ten thousand dreams burst forth.

Gold summer's breeze glides round.
She moves her silken gown to catch its touch
On breast and thigh. Her rouged cheeks glow.
Pressed close, her lover sings ten thousand songs,
Ten thousand kisses gives,
Ten thousand dreams fulfills.

Gray autumn's frost creeps round.
Dead leaves lie brittle on the sunless bench.
War parts the lovers, chills her heart,
Turns her garden upside down, stills her songs.
Ten thousand tears she cries,
Ten thousand dreams forgets.

White winter's snow swirls round.
She clasps her brocade gown across her breast.
Cold moonlight shines in rouge stained tears.
Far from her bed, her lover dies. She waits
Ten thousand lonely nights,
Ten thousand silent years.

The song wove around them. No one moved. The pine log crackled. Finally, her grandfather touched her arm. His hand trembled. "Mai, how do you know that song?"

"I'm not sure," she said as she let her hands fall from the bowl. "It was a memory. It seemed to come from the bowl."

Her grandfather stared at her. Slowly, he straightened his back. "Slide the bowl this way. Let me look," he said quietly.

"What will you see, I wonder?" she said.

"Duty," he said with certainty.

Again Mai felt a sharp shock of electricity when her fingers touched the bowl and her grandfather's hands visibly jerked as he clasped the bowl, although he did not hesitate to wrap his fingers tightly around it.

The pine log flared, burning brightly. Red flames flickered momentarily on the surface of the water, then moved deep inside the bowl. His fingers shifted the bowl, ever so slightly. The water eddied. Her grandfather stared straight down. "I see yarrow stalks. Swirling." He leaned closer.

Mai stared at the water. A peacock appeared, upside down, its feet on the surface of the water, its head on the bottom of the bowl. Willow leaves and clouds gathered in the bottom. It was the garden, upside down, without a woman in it. Then she saw a stream of fire.

Her grandfather must have seen it too. "Danger! There is fire. Shadows. A man holding a sword." His voice was a deep tone Mai had never heard before. Her eyes darted between his face and the water searching for that vision.

The water increased its spin, wildly swirled for several seconds until it became a vortex beating violently against the sides of the bowl. Silver beams of light flashed across the vortex. Her grandfather shouted in Chinese,

"Quickly, we must flee. Now!" With a sharp cry he fell forward. Mai had never seen him faint. Fear tightened her throat. Flames from the pine log colored the water a deep blood red.

Angelo rose to his knees. "Stop it. Stop the water."

As Mai thrust out her hand to grab the bowl, another crack of electricity hit her. She pushed through the pain and slammed her arm against the bowl. Waves spilled across the table and cascaded to the floor. Mai's grandfather gripped the edge of the table and pushed himself away from it. All three of them stared, stunned, at a simple, small puddle of water on the white carpet.

"What the hell was that?" Angelo said.

"Are you all right, Grandfather?"

Her grandfather lifted the bowl to his chest. Tension strained his voice. He spoke so slowly that Mai feared he was blacking out. "This is an oracle bowl. There is great danger here."

James came in. "What's going on? Why the shouting?"

After they stood, Mai described the event. James said, "Are you all sure you didn't hallucinate on *yiin miao* tea while I was in the study?"

"There was no *yiin miao* tea. What happened was quite real," Mai said, irritated and still shaken. Angelo put his arm around her shoulder.

"I'll take you at your word," James said.

"There is great danger here," Mai's grandfather said again. "I must take the bowl."

"I understand the urgency you feel, Daniel. I also think you should leave right away with the bowl. I'll get you both on a plane as soon as I can get you a visa. Mai's travel documents are always in place."

"Then I need to wait for the visa at home in San Francisco," Mai's grandfather said, "with the bowl in my bank safe-deposit box."

"I'll take you now," Mai said.

"No, I want you as far away from the bowl as possible. You stay to finish your obligations at Coconut Gallery."

"I can ask Louis to carry on without me."

"No."

"Let's do this," James said. "It's late. Put the bowl back in my safe. In the morning I'll do the necessary court business from my Monterey office. Then I'll take Daniel to San Francisco."

Mai kissed her grandfather's cheek. She felt the slightest trembling on his skin. Although his voice was steady, he was not calm. Neither was her stomach. It was with great reluctance that she said goodbye and she and Angelo walked outside.

In the night sky the Milky Way appeared as a stable, sparkling river, in high contrast to their whirling, fleeting visions in the bowl. Mai backed the Jaguar into a level area just big enough to turn the car around and headed slowly up the driveway. The security gate rattled open as they turned to look back at the starlit hillside.

"Whatever destiny is in those stars," Mai said, "I'm not feeling good about it."

FRIDAY

27

A SPIDER

The next morning, Friday, Mai conducted her scheduled Chinese brush painting demonstration at Coconut Gallery for a small group of patrons. Afterwards, she met Angelo and together they walked to Custom House Plaza. She carried an easel and he had a two-by-three foot canvas tucked under one arm. The cargo crate camera obscura glistened with fresh gold paint, smelled of new wood, and had THIS SIDE UP stenciled in crimson on the back.

Mai was wearing a yellow Valentino sundress, one she usually wore on vacation, one that outwardly conveyed a certain air of happiness and hope even though inside she felt deeply worried about her grandfather. Angelo wore an indigo Armani shirt, a color neither blue nor violet, and Mai sensed from it his anxiety and stress. He was definitely somewhere between blue and violet.

Angelo's crew assembled the scaffolding. They banged hammers and wielded high-speed drills which squealed from the top of the Custom House. A giant structure took shape. It looked like a spider with tall legs stretched down from the two story end sections and shorter legs crouched in front of the single story middle section. The tarantula legs were firmly rooted in temporary steel bases. The structure would support the drapery and allow it to fall gracefully around, but not touch, the historic building. Walkways at the top of each of the three sections allowed workers to stand inside the spider. From there they would drop the drapery to engulf the building.

One of the workmen shouted from the scaffolding. "Hey, Angelo, just so you know. We might not get this done by tomorrow morning."

"Just get it done by high noon," Angelo shouted back. "Or the TV cameras and flashbulbs will capture your face, not mine, registering failure." He waved the canvas at him and laughed. "In spite of everything, I feel good this morning."

"I know," she said. He was the most resilient person she knew. "Who are all those people up there on the walkway?" she asked. Bob-The-Critic led a line of seven people with cameras. Second in line was Toni Wilson. Mai felt a threat from high on the tarantula.

"Bob's press people," Angelo said, without glancing up. "He's leading a docent tour, so to speak." He shifted the canvas to his other hand.

"Hey, mister." A boy of about seven confronted Angelo. "What are you doing with that white square?"

"This, young man, is artist canvas." He placed his hand on his chest. "And I am an artist."

The boy put his hands on his hips, clearly offended. "Duh. I know that. But what are you doing?"

"See this little building that looks like a cargo crate?

I'm making a moving picture show inside it."

"How?"

The sailmaker came up and handed Angelo an electric drill. "The cloth will be finished by tonight. Get this contraption ready."

Angelo nodded, took the drill, and looked again at the boy.

"How, indeed?"

"Explain it to him, please," the boy's mother said. "It will make my life so much easier."

"Well, young man. Stand over here. You see that wall of the cargo crate? Now turn around. You see the Custom House?" The boy made the turns as did his sister, mother, and a few suntanned tourists.

Angelo flourished the drill like a pistol.

"I drill a hole right there." He pointed the drill at the side wall of the camera obscura. "And I place this canvas inside opposite the hole. All this sunlight pours through that tiny hole and hits my canvas and brings the Custom House inside." He lowered his voice and bent down to the boy. "Only guess what."

"What?" the boy whispered back.

"On my canvas, the Custom House is upside down."

"No way."

"Tell you what." He was talking to the crowd as well as the boy. "You come tomorrow. Your mom can stand here. You can come inside. You'll see your mom upside down, I promise." He raised his voice even louder. "Tomorrow, you all can come inside and see things upside down."

Mai heard Angelo but her attention was on Bob who led the seven people along the walkway at the top of the tarantula. That bug of foreboding which she first felt in Locke stomped in an ever tightening circle around her chest because, high above, Toni Wilson walked very close behind Bob, her hand touching his back.

28

SPIDER WEBS

Sitting in the breakfast nook of Casa de Chang's kitchen, Daniel Sung made a series of phone calls to alert his hospital staff about his departure to China. He hoped music and food would calm his nerves, so he put Beethoven in the CD player and whisked three eggs with some of the Parmesan cheese and basil from last night's feast. While the omelet sizzled, he made tea in a black pot painted with white chrysanthemums.

He carried the plate and a fork in one hand and balanced a teacup on top of the teapot in the other hand and got all to the table on the deck without a mishap.

The scent of kelp from the sea and the music lightened his dark mood. Above, the sun's rays battled a few cloud dragons. Below, the peacock lumbered through the garden, swishing its long plumes over strawberry plants as it looked for snails.

When Daniel finished eating, he walked down the cobblestones alongside the house to weed the garden in the company of the peacock. Farther down, coming from the deep shade of the pines and cypress trees, a rustling and crunching of leaves caught his attention. He turned his head towards the lowest terrace.

It had been deer last night.

Three blacktail deer were nibbling shoots of grass, two outside the barely visible wire fence in the neighboring yard, one inside the yard of Casa de Chang. He put his hand in front of the taut neck of the peacock so it would not follow and moved silently down the stone stairs to the middle terrace.

The deer in the yard raised its head, panicked, and ran hard into the fence several times before it stopped, frozen in fear, against the farthest corner of the fence. It couldn't find the opening.

Daniel moved slowly down the next set of stone stairs, inch by inch, his foot suspended over each stair for seconds before his heel touched. From the last stone step he could see the break in the fence to his left. With the same quiet glide he walked across leaves and pine needles to the opening in the fence.

The fence was cut.

The wire had been sliced down one post, pulled out, and rolled back on itself. He puzzled about that as he removed the rock that held it back and rolled the wire all the way to the next post, creating a larger opening. He'd asked James about the cut. Then he walked silently back to the stone stairs and climbed to the second terrace where he sat down on the wall and remained without moving. The deer darted out of the corner, looked farther down the hill toward the other two deer, butted against the fence three times before it came to the wide opening and finally escaped.

Daniel breathed in relief and eased off the wall. He climbed leisurely towards the garden terrace behind the swish swish of the peacock's tail. When he was halfway up the path, he heard the snap of a twig. The peacock's neck straightened as its head twisted around. Its eyes darted. Daniel jerked his head to the left just in time to see the gun before he felt the cold, hard barrel jam into his ribs.

"Keep walking old man, all the way into the house where you keep old bowls." It was a voice as clear as sunlight but as cold as the gun barrel. Daniel instantly suspected that he was the Italian smuggler that James and Mai had talked about.

The gun pressed hard into Daniel's side and threw his balance off as he walked up the hill. He opened his hand and tensed his arm in preparation for an attempt to disarm the man and stepped ever so slightly to the side ready to spin away from the gun. But the peacock rushed alongside him and turned sharply against his leg. He lost his balance and fell forward on his knees.

"I could blow this little bird brain away if you like," Frank Conti said, turning the pistol on the peacock.

"No need," Daniel said. He regained his balance and stood. "That little bird brain is not a very good witness." He kept his weight off one foot, poised to kick the gun out of the hand.

Conti jumped out of range of Daniel's leg and aimed the gun in his face. "Before you try that stupid kung fu kicking stuff, look carefully at this little cell phone transmission."

Conti held up the small screen of a cell phone. On it, Mai and Angelo walked side by side in Custom House Plaza. "If you look closely, you will see one of my friends directly behind your granddaughter. You can't see his gun but I'll tell you, he's a very good shot." Conti held the screen with one hand and, at arm's length, pressed the gun into Daniel Sung's stomach.

"Are you sure the whole image of the Custom House will project through a small hole onto that canvas?" Mai asked.

"We'll find out." Angelo opened the sliding door and they entered the camera obscura, careful not to brush against the wet paint. The room was hot and reeked with paint fumes.

Mai arranged the easel's three legs and positioned it by the back wall. Angelo set the drill down and propped the canvas on the easel. "This has to work," he said quickly, as if the four words were one, too excited to pause between words.

"I bet it works perfectly." She felt a good excitement for the first time in days. She suspected Angelo had been in this room several times already and knew exactly where he wanted to drill the hole that would let the bright sunlight in to project the outside scene onto the canvas.

Angelo squatted, held the drill up, and pulled the trigger, testing to make sure the drill was charged. The high pitch of the whir said it was. He put his finger on the spot midway up the wall. "Okay, I'm ready."

Mai slid the door shut. The construction of the small eight-by-ten room was excellent. No light entered from outside. Angelo nudged the drill against his finger marking the spot and pressed the bit into the wood.

"Ready? Set? Go." He pulled the trigger and removed the drill from the small hole.

Outside colors and shapes spilled into the room.

"All right," Angelo said. "Now let's find the best spot for the canvas." He picked up the canvas and walked it close to the hole, then back a little, watching the images on it. He held it over his head and then in front of his legs. "What do you think?" he asked Mai.

She moved the easel to the middle of the room about four feet from the hole. "Put it here."

The Custom House tarantula was on its back with its legs pointed to the ceiling in relatively clear focus on the canvas. Elsewhere around the room, the images on the walls and ceiling were not so sharp and the corners of the room remained dim. Still, blue sky spread out on the floor and fuzzy tourists moved upside down across the back wall.

"Move the easel toward the hole a little more," Angelo said. "See if the Custom House is clearer."

She moved the easel forward. "No," she said, peering over the top of the canvas. "I think it's better where it was."

"Right. So do I."

"Whoa," Mai shouted. "What was that?"

A dark form tumbled from the tarantula at the bottom of the canvas and rolled up and off the canvas to the ceiling.

"I don't know," Angelo cried. "Something outside. Quick, open the door."

Outside, the construction crew and Bob's tour people looked down from the center section walkway. Tourists looked up. Everyone screamed.

Bob-The-Critic, screaming louder than anyone, dangled in the air, one foot bound in coils of rope which held him swaying just three feet from the base of the Custom House. Mai pushed through the crowd.

"Robert." She caught him on a down swing and held him in her arms. His eyes were wide. A white hardhat was still anchored firmly to his head by a strap under his chin.

From above, someone yelled, "He tripped in the rigging."

Saliva flowed out of the corners of Bob's mouth. "I did not trip. I was pushed. Pushed! Help. Help. Someone hit my back. Pushed. Pushed."

"Stop babbling," Mai said, readjusting his body, tightening her arms, and lifting him to give the rope some slack. "We have you." Angelo pulled at the rope trying to uncoil it from Bob's ankle which jutted at an alarming angle.

Construction workers climbed down the scaffold while a hundred people shouted and a fire truck zoomed onto the plaza.

Mai looked at Angelo. She saw the panic in his eyes.

"I'm toast," Angelo said. "A broken critic in the midst of my art project. Hell. That's almost as disastrous as a bad review."

Mai couldn't smile at his weird humor because welling up from her stomach was the nausea of fear. She raised Bob so that Angelo could unwind the rope without pulling off his ankle.

"Pushed. Mai. I was pushed." There were tears in his eyes.

"You'll be fine, Robert." Mai spoke like an impatient

mother. "That fall was very dramatic. Your picture on the news will be impressive. Look. Your carnation is still in your lapel."

Robert swallowed. As if seeking comfort, his eyes searched Mai's face. Instead, she offered a warning. "You might not want to give the fireman that explanation unless you have a really good reason why Toni Wilson might have pushed you. Do you? Are you in league with smugglers?"

Seemingly in the throes of a new panic attack, Robert twitched as Mai handed him over to a fireman.

Mai and Angelo hastily threaded their way out of the crowd. "He was pushed, Angelo. No doubt. I bet Toni sent him to buy the bowl from Cypress. And she sent Conti to Carmel to pick it up. Conti must have told her he saw me escape with it. She saw you in the EastWest Art Gallery and thought you were arranging to sell the bowl. She probably had Bob search your studio for it."

"Pushing him off the scaffolding is a pretty strong way to tell him not to blab if Edna or Helen summons the police," Angelo said.

Mai felt a riptide of fear pull her under. "Go make sure Cypress is safe. I'm going to Grandfather."

29

LOSS

"Move to the house," Frank Conti demanded. Daniel Sung moved his ribcage to the side to relieve the pressure of the gun barrel and weighed his options. Mai might be safe. Crowds filled the Plaza. He took a hesitant step upward towards the house.

Conti rammed the gun deeper and raised the cell screen. "I am deadly serious. Don't try anything."

On the tiny screen, he again saw Mai.

"Nice resolution for a small screen, don't you think?" Conti said.

The small image of Mai was devastating. He could not risk her. He had lived a lifetime without fulfilling his obligation to the bowl. He could wait many more years if he had to.

Daniel Sung entered the house and walked across the shadows on the sparkling floor to the long hallway. Each step he took measured out the bowl's years from the Zhou Dynasty when an artist carved enigmatic images on a small water mirror, to a thirteenth century tavern where a sing-song girl recognized the bowl from the lyrics of a song and gave it to a monk, to son after son after son for another thousand years. Step by step the years trailed behind him as he approached the safe hidden in the linen closet. When he pulled the bowl from that secret place, loss overwhelmed him. He bowed his head and steadied himself with one hand on the wall.

Frank Conti ripped the bowl from his grasp. It was such a sudden, savage gesture that anger flashed through him. Daniel thrust his knee into Conti's groin and yanked at the bowl with both hands but was unable to wrest it from him.

"You stupid old man," Conti screamed. He punched his gun hand into Daniel's stomach, hard, and then shoved him to the front door. "Open the security gate," Conti said. "One more move and I use a bullet instead of a fist."

Daniel could hardly breathe and his stomach cramped in pain. At the front door he had to touch the switch twice before the security gate rattled open.

Outside, Frank Conti stared up the driveway as if anticipating a car. Daniel moved slightly to Conti's left and kept his shoulder towards the lower terraces. He also stared up the driveway, forcing his eyes to be calm and his face serene in order to distract Conti from what he saw out of the corner of his eye. A strange man in a Hawaiian shirt was working his way up the terraces from the deer fence.

"Drop the gun, Conti, or I'll drop you." Hunter shouted dramatically, in spite of a winded breathiness in his voice. Holding a gun at arm's length, he aimed at Conti.

"Who the hell are you?" Conti said, turning slightly toward Hunter but aiming the gun directly at Daniel Sung's chest.

"The rightful owner of that bowl," Hunter said. "Hand it over."

"Yeah, right, bozo. My bullet hits the old man before you catch your breath enough to squeeze the trigger."

Daniel looked back and forth at each man. One had to be Frank Conti. The other one with two splinted fingers might be Mai's Hunter.

Danger.

He shuddered. Blood red water swirled in his memory. He felt a sharp pain in his throat, the same pain he felt last night when he stared into the oracle bowl.

No one moved.

Except the peacock. In a flash of color and a rush of wind from wings, the great hulk of the peacock swooped down from the pine tree. Its sharp claws raked Conti's chest. Conti threw both arms across his face to protect himself. The gun stayed gripped in his hand, but the bowl zinged into the midst of a frantic swirl of flapping wings, darting claws, and striking beak.

Conti dodged and crouched to get away from the peacock. He staggered towards the strawberries.

Hunter kneed the peacock out of his way, grabbed the bowl, and, without missing a beat, fired three bullets into the dirt by Conti. The peacock screeched.

Hunter screamed, "Drop the gun."

Daniel, shaking, felt his body weaken. All this was his fault. He saw no way to end the combat. He took a step backwards.

Frank Conti, still stumbling, swiveled and fired the

gun, hitting Hunter in the leg. Hunter shot back just as Conti pulled the trigger a second time. That bullet hit Daniel Sung.

30

FINDING CYPRESS

Angelo barged into Carmel Floral Treasures. Something was wrong. He didn't know what. But something was not the way it usually was.

"Cypress. Cypress," he called, rushing through the beaded curtain. The office was empty. He opened the back door. The van was parked in its spot behind the shop. He went again to the front. The tubs of flowers, baker's rack of pots, everything was in place.

Maybe he and Mai overreacted.

No. Something was wrong.

He inhaled. No sweet flag. He spun around. The matches were in the tall holder with incense sticks beside them. Nothing was burning. Cypress never opened the shop for business without lighting the sweet flag.

Angelo darted into the deli next to Carmel Floral Treasures. "Archie, did you see Cypress open the shop this morning?"

"Hi, Angelo. Sure. She said she'd bring me fresh flowers but she hasn't come back yet. To tell the truth, though, she looked more than a little out of it."

More than a little out of it. Oh, God. He knew that look. And he knew where it took her, unexpectedly, at odd hours. She was in danger, but not from Toni Wilson or Frank Conti. He ran.

The beach was crowded. Angelo knew Cypress would see no one. She would walk in a trance, alone on that picture perfect sand until the dark body washed ashore. A boy. No more than one year old.

Whenever she walked along this white sand, that body was there. She'd pick it up, carry it back into the sea, get it out of her path. Only then could she walk on.

Angelo waded into the waves, knee deep beside her. He had to be careful not to alarm her, wake her too quickly. "Cypress," he called gently, taking her hand.

She turned her head. Angelo's black hair and wet indigo shirt seemed to surprise her. Color against the white sand.

"What do you want?" she said.

He couldn't tell if she recognized him. "To be sure you are okay."

A wave lifted his feet an inch off the sandy bottom. When he touched down, he guided her out of the water to a space on the beach. "Please, Cypress. Sit for just a minute."

She sank to the sand, but her eyes stared out to sea. He spoke again, so softly he was afraid she wouldn't hear him. "Where are you, Cypress?"

"On the beach. Where I always am." She dug her toes into the sand. Her eyes focused on him with effort, finally recognizing him. "What are you doing here?"

"Mai and I were worried about you. Toni Wilson pushed Bob off the Custom House. He could have died."

"Like that boy, there, on the beach."

Angelo wrapped his arms around her. "There is no boy there, Cypress. He is gone."

"I know. He is dead. He died in a car crash."

"Yes. He is dead. And he is gone. You will not find him again." He held her tight.

Cypress wrapped her arms around her knees, rocking a little, still trapped in the past. "Angelo, how did you get involved with someone like Walter?"

"I don't know. It just happened." He put his hand on her knee to stop the rocking.

"Why did it happen?"

"Why do you walk on this beach looking for our son? We cannot find him ever again. Come away from here, Cypress."

She shook her head. "In a minute. You worry too much. Toni Wilson won't push me off anything." Cypress put her hand on Angelo's face. "You be careful."

31

THE PEACOCK CRIED

Mai's heart, already pounding loudly, boomed to thunder when she saw Casa de Chang's security gate wide open and heard the peacock crying.

She jammed on the brakes at the bottom of the driveway. Just beyond the arbor, the peacock stood over a body, its iridescent neck swaying, its tail plumes fanned wide, its plaintive voice raised again and again.

Mai ran from the car and knelt beside the body of her grandfather. Bright blood covered his face, hair, neck, and shoulders. His whole face seemed torn apart. She thought she saw white bone protruding from the blood on his left cheek. She bent close, listening for breath and felt only a hint of pulse at his neck.

"I called 911."

The voice startled her. She jerked her head away from her grandfather's face. She couldn't form words. Tears rushed down her cheeks. Hunter sat propped against a pine tree, covered with dirt, his right leg rigid, blood soaking his pant leg.

"I called 911." He struggled to tighten his belt as a tourniquet around his thigh. A short distance from him was the body of Frank Conti.

"He's dead," Hunter said through clenched teeth. "I shot him."

Mai managed to shake herself into action. She ran into the house, emerged seconds later, and threw a towel to Hunter. She folded another and gently pressed it against her grandfather's cheek to stop the bleeding. It seemed a lifetime before she could speak. "Tell me what happened."

Hunter's lips stretched in thin strips of pain as he pressed the towel with all his might against his leg. He winced. "I followed Conti. He climbed the hill. I sat on my bike behind his car on the street down there." Hunter hardly moved his mouth. Mai strained to hear him. "When he didn't come back down, I came up. The three of us wrestled for the bowl. I grabbed it." His voice faded away.

"Hunter. Don't stop talking. Stay awake."

Mai barely heard him say, "I blacked out. Came to. Called 911." He sucked in air. "Can we talk later? I'm not so good."

Mai could hear him struggling for breath as much as she was. Her grandfather barely breathed at all. He was dying.

"Hunter?" It was a desperate plea.

With what must have been a supreme effort, Hunter jammed his left elbow into the ground and pulled his body along until he was within arm's length of her. He brushed her tears away. "It's okay. The ambulance is coming down the driveway now."

Her relief lasted half a second. A thought crashed into her.

"Where's the bowl?"

32

THE BAMBOO GROVE

The confinement of the hospital waiting room scraped on Mai's nerves. Hours after she found her grandfather, he was still in surgery. Hunter slept sedated in the recovery room. His leg, fractured by the bullet, was in a long cast. James Chang dealt with the police at the crime scene.

Mai walked outside to the coffee stand. Came back in with coffee. Walked outside for a muffin. Came back in. Sat. Picked up a magazine. Couldn't read. Couldn't sit. Paced. Sat.

Outside, wisps of fog flowed in currents of evening air. Mai wandered away from the hospital down a path to a grove of bamboo which screened the cement parking structure. The thick bamboo stalks offered a sturdy comfort. A tiny wren hopped around her feet, little black eyes alert for a handout. She had no muffin crumbs to toss. Her stomach hurt.

In the last few months she barely thought of her grandfather at all. Now overwhelming sadness brought him back, the same sadness that had encased her after her mother and father died when she was five. Only her grandfather's strong arms wrapped tight around her month after month had drawn her out of her fear of being all alone, abandoned. What would she do without him?

Angelo sat down beside her. "I couldn't find you inside. Are you okay?" He took her hand.

"I think so." She lied.

"You aren't answering your phone. I called James. He explained."

"Sorry. I'm really worried. Is Cypress all right?"

"Fine. Well, fine for her."

"She's like bamboo. Bends but doesn't break." She held his hand tightly, glad about Cypress.

James Chang walked to them, shook Angelo's hand and hugged Mai, his face very close to hers. She noticed stress lines in his usually smooth face. "I've talked to the trauma surgeon," he said.

A new wave of fear swept over Mai. He must have felt her shoulders contract for he tightened his arm around her and spoke quietly. "The worst is over. The bullet shattered his cheek but the plastic surgeon will be able to reconstruct his face." He waited. "I'm afraid they couldn't save his eye."

At first Mai felt great relief, then great horror. She imagined her grandfather waking to that reality. "He won't be able to work as a surgeon. He's always cared for others."

"And he still will." James kept his arm around her.

"Do you want some soup or something from the cafeteria?" Angelo asked.

"No. Not now. You two go in. I'll walk a little."

The gently curving path wandered through the bamboo. She walked slowly, feeling hopeful.

Then she remembered the bowl. Where was it?

At Casa de Chang, Hunter told her only that he grabbed the bowl. But he blacked out just as the ambulance arrived and couldn't say more.

Why was there no trace of it? While the paramedics worked on Hunter and her grandfather, she scoured the arbor, dug among the strawberry plants of the terrace, and sifted through pine needles, her heart racing. The bowl was not there.

When she stood holding her grandfather's hand while the paramedics lifted him into the ambulance, fear that he would die pushed the bowl from her thoughts. But here her grandfather was safe in the hands of the surgeons. She had nothing to do but think and his bowl pushed its way back into her thoughts.

Along with the rustle of the bamboo leaves, the bowl's song played in her head, the same melody for each of the four seasons. If she sang it again and again, spring would always come around bringing another chance for life. Her grandfather would survive even though his bowl was lost.

Her pace became uneven. The Sung family bowl. How many sons had died without fulfilling the strange destiny? Return a lost bowl to an unknown temple. The burden of ancestors.

Her breath caught in her throat. She stopped. With sudden insight, she knew. Her grandfather was the last son to hear the story of the bowl but not the last child. This bowl was no longer her grandfather's burden. It was hers. Her destiny. It was she who had to return the oracle's bowl to the temple, fill it with yarrow stalks, make it part of the future.

Where was it? Who took it from the pools of blood at Casa de Chang? She wiped her hands across the blood stains on her yellow sundress.

As she paced back and forth in the bamboo grove, she remembered the vortex of water in the oracle bowl last night. What had it revealed? Upside down images. A stream of fire. She stopped dead. *That's it. Upside down images, the counterpart of reality. A stream of fire. Metal flowing from a crucible. The creation of a bowl, a negative bowl. A forgery.*

She bolted out of the bamboo grove. In the waiting room she found James and Angelo. "I have to go. Please stay until you are certain that Grandfather is all right."

James and Angelo both looked shocked. "Where are you going?"

"To Toni Wilson's studio foundry."

"Do you think she has the bowl in San Francisco?" James asked.

"Of course she does," Mai said. "Why was I so stupid?"

"She's dangerous," Angelo blurted.

"I have to go. Alone. James, don't send anyone else. This is for me to do."

33

THE FOUNDRY

The streets at the west end of Golden Gate Park were shrouded in fog and darkness. Mai couldn't see the white center line on the road or the one at the edge marking the bicycle lane, couldn't keep the Jaguar in her lane. She was racing to find Toni, getting nowhere, the hands on the dashboard clock sweeping away minutes. She'd been pent up in the hospital until her whole body twitched. Now she was locked in this black fog. It made her crazy. Her chest hurt. Her head spun.

She leaned her head out the window, straining to see beyond the flapping windshield wipers. Her left front tire bumped against the curb. She gave up. She could make her way on foot faster than this. Grabbing the belt that held her hunting knife from the glove compartment, she abandoned the car on the wrong side of the road. While she tightened the knife's belt around her waist, she tried to figure out exactly where she was. She couldn't see any lights. She couldn't hear the surf. She must still be blocks away from the sea.

She kept one of her sandals curled over the rim of the curb as a guide and walked as fast as she could. She smacked into the corner of a dark transit kiosk.

"Where am I?" She was frustrated, talking out loud. Rubbing her scraped forehead, she squinted, searching up and down the street. "I can't see a thing. Why is the power off?"

She groped the buildings as she walked. Finally her hand rubbed across a glass window. She stopped. She knew where she was. This was the neighborhood market several blocks from Toni's studio. She walked faster.

At last she reached the sea. Long bands of glowing light stretched up and down the coast, eerily luminescent in the fog hanging over the waves. The red tide's tiny organisms sparkled, ebbed and flowed in the ocean's easy motion. When she'd enjoyed the display Tuesday on her evening run, hundreds of cars filled the beach lots. Now all was strangely empty. Why? The power outage? Road closures? Whatever the reason, the unexpected emptiness grated against her already strained nerves, reinforcing her fear that Toni's studio would be empty and the bowl already spirited out of the city.

In the sea's light, Mai ran the short distance to the two story warehouse which was Toni's ocean view studio. No cars were parked in front. She rattled the front door. A bolt held it tight. A metal shutter secured the only window. A gull screeched a sinister warning. A burst of panic tightened her throat. Maybe she was wrong. How the hell would she find Toni if she wasn't here?

Before her thoughts slipped into total chaos, she dashed around the building to look for a back way in. The loading dock where Toni moved big statues out of the studio was also empty. Mai swiped her hand over the wet metal of the tall garage door, feeling for a handle. There was none. Stepping backwards, looking for another way in, she saw a flickering of light. At first she thought it was the moon fighting to escape the fog. Instead, the glow came from a second story window by the fire escape. She exhaled. The studio was not deserted. Someone was in there.

She stretched her hands high and pulled down the fire escape ladder. Each hard rung of the ladder cut into her thin-soled sandals as she climbed. At the top she tried to lift the center board of the window. The glass pane rattled, but the weathered board stuck tight. Pulling the knife from its sheath, she pried the latch off and inched the window up. The saturated wood scraped and squealed. She caught her breath, listened for an alarm. Hearing nothing, she crawled through onto a narrow catwalk.

Warm air brushed her face. Kaleidoscopic lights jerked across the dark interior. Mai held her breath. She had expected neither warmth nor bizarre lighting. Cautiously she crept to the railing.

She clenched the railing. Toni was down there. Her shadow danced in flickering light. Mai heard hissing gas jets and saw fire behind the open hatch in the side of a large furnace. Fire. That was the source of the erratic light.

Danger.

Her grandfather's cry and her vision of fire in the oracle bowl whipped through her head.

Mai moved quickly to her right along the catwalk, closer to the furnace wall, analyzing the room of alternating dark shadows and bright flickers. Toni's car was parked below her, just inside the garage door. In front of it, in the middle of the room, a two foot, cone shaped granite crucible hung several feet off the floor, suspended from a track and pulley system anchored to the ceiling. A long rod leaned at an angle against the crucible.

Without power, the crucible could not be pulled along the track, neither lowered through a hatch in the top of the furnace nor lifted out. None of the brick size bars of bronze stacked under the crucible could be melted tonight.

Maybe the oracle bowl's vision was wrong. No stream of fire would make a duplicate bowl tonight. She was somewhat relieved. If she had thought for a moment in the hospital she would have remembered that the process of making a bowl would take at least a week. Power or no power, her mad dash and panic were not necessary.

Mai blinked away tiny drops of sweat which blurred her eyes. Toni couldn't pour bronze tonight. Then why was she here? Maybe she was using the flames as an emergency source of light. To do what?

Something Edna had said tugged at her memory. The manager of the EastWest Art Gallery wanted to buy the bowl. Of course. An immediate sale. Toni was waiting for a buyer. She had the bowl with her. Where?

Mai's eyes fully adjusted to the odd light and she carefully surveyed the room below. The street entrance was to her left opposite the catwalk. One of Toni's finished statues, a tall, bony bronze skeleton, stood in a display space near the entrance. Against the wall opposite the catwalk was a long workbench.

Mai saw a small glow on the workbench. She squinted. Reflections of red furnace flames circled the curves of a bowl. Its shape was unmistakable. Her bowl. Here. She almost shouted for joy.

She didn't. The light which circled the bowl reflected off the barrel of a gun lying next to it.

Danger.

Again her grandfather's voice echoed in her head. Toni's shadow twitched on the wall. Mai tightened her grip on her knife, a very inadequate weapon. But the memory of her grandfather lying on the ground covered in blood flared inside her. She had to get down there fast.

Clutching the knife, she ran along the catwalk away from the furnace towards the stairs at the opposite end. The metal catwalk swayed slightly, jingled. In spite of the sound, she kept moving. Tall shelves stacked with boxes left little room for her to squeeze by. She was careless. Her sandal caught on the edge of one of the shelves. She fell against it. A box tumbled off. She managed to catch it before it tumbled down the stairs but her scuffling noises seemed thunderous. She didn't wait for Toni to react, didn't waste a second.

From the top stair she shouted, "Don't move one inch, Toni." She pointed the handle of the knife like a gun barrel at Toni and flew down the stairs, expecting Toni to charge for the gun on the workbench halfway between her and Toni. Instead, Toni's jaw dropped with a loud intake of air. She fumbled with something on the workbench and, strangely, backed away from the workbench, facing Mai.

Mai raced across the room from stairs to workbench as Toni inched backward towards the crucible in the center of the room. Knife in one hand, Mai grabbed the gun with the other and pointed it at Toni. With fury in her voice, she yelled, "You picked this bowl out of a pool of my grandfather's blood."

"Wait. Wait, Mai. You have it all wrong." Toni shouted above the hiss of the gas jets in the furnace and held up one hand for Mai to stop. She whined. "I didn't know he was your grandfather. I don't know how everyone got shot. All I know is Frank told me he would steal the bowl and I had to pick him up."

Tony's voice, full of denial, ripped into Mai. She could hardly listen.

Toni took another step backwards. "Honestly, Mai, the security gate was wide open like Frank said it would be. So I drove in to pick him up. I only went there to pick up Frank."

"You had no trouble picking up the bowl." Anger overcame Mai. Her hands shook, her pulse throbbed against her throat. Toni was a weasel. She wanted to smash her. She yelled, "Stop moving backwards. Stand still!"

Toni stopped close to the crucible. "Believe me. I panicked. I really panicked. Three bodies on the ground, no one moving, no one conscious. A peacock dashing around. I didn't know what to do. Honestly, the bowl wasn't anywhere near your grandfather. It was just sitting there next to Hunter. I picked it up and left as fast as I could. But you take it now. Just take it."

"What?" That easy surrender of the bowl incensed Mai even more. Had all that blood spilled for so casual a theft? Heat burned inside her as if the furnace flames were within her. Sweat blurred her eyes. She lost concentration. Her hands shook.

Toni took a sudden step away from the crucible. A long silver rod, one of the furnace tools, flashed like a sword in her hand.

Mai pulled the trigger. The bullet ricocheted off the crucible. Mai felt the kick of the gun in her hand, heard the squeal of the bullet. Startled, she shook her head, throwing off droplets of sweat, suddenly aware that she had lost control. The gun hung loose in one hand.

At that instant Toni slammed the rod into Mai's arm. Pain spiked up to her shoulder. The gun tore from her hand and scraped along the floor clanging to a stop against the metal garage door.

Toni slashed at Mai again.

Mai saw the flash of silver. She regained control. She dodged. She spun a sharp kick into Toni's hip and knocked her into the suspended granite crucible. The rod clattered on the floor. The crucible moved slightly backward with Toni plastered against it. Her body momentarily stayed on the crucible, then toppled off.

Mai wheeled around to find out why Toni backed away from the workbench. Two halves of a mold lay open on the workbench, impressions of her ancestor's bowl. Toni must have worked all afternoon making this mold.

Next to the mold, in a tub of water, a dark red bowl floated, a wax bowl, protected from the heat in cold water, in no danger of sagging. A wax bowl, an exact copy of her bowl, created when Toni poured hot wax into the mold.

This was what Toni didn't want her to find, the potential for many future bowls. A master mold. From it wax bowls would be made, wax bowls which would be covered with clay and fired in the kiln. Wax bowls which would melt away leaving hard ceramic shells into which bronze would be poured. Many bowls from one master mold. Forged. Sold.

None of that would happen. Mai hurled the two halves of the mold into the fires of the furnace. Black smoke spewed out. She lifted the wax bowl, dripping with cold water, and slammed it onto the workbench. Again and again she pounded it with the blunt handle of her knife as if it were both Frank Conti and Toni Wilson. She flattened the wax bowl, pressed the distorted pieces hard into the workbench so that nothing remained except a thin band of dark red wax already beginning to melt in the heat of the room.

She replaced the knife in its sheath on her belt, anchored the real bowl against her ribs with her left arm, and sprinted around the bony bronze skeleton to the entrance. When she turned the knob and pulled, the door held tight. Her right fingers fumbled for a deadbolt latch and twisted it. She yanked the door open.

Toni's shout echoed in the midst of a gun shot. "I'll get you, Mai Ling." A bullet splintered the doorjamb.

Surprise stopped Mai cold. She turned. Through the rib cage of the skeleton she saw Toni at the front fender of the car, gun in hand.

34

INTO THE RIVER

Mai darted across the deserted street outside Toni's studio. The fog still hung above the sea. In it the moon was a fuzzy presence, its diffused light casting no shadows. A foghorn blasted harsh warnings. Haloed lights on a freighter, like tiny lanterns on bamboo poles, bobbed on the sea. Just north, up the steep hill, the deserted Cliff House restaurant loomed, a fortress above the sea. Beyond that, cloistered in a small canyon, the ruins of the former Sutro Baths sulked at sea level, cold shells of once warm swimming pools. On the hills beyond the ruins, pines and cypress. Mai needed to get to those trees and the safety of her house.

Mai was a strong runner, but Toni would be right behind her. In the open with no cover, she angled from the center of the street to the wall separating the pavement from beach sand. Panting, she looked behind for Toni. She saw no one.

Without stopping to rest, she ran up the sidewalk parallel to the wall, zigzagging to make a poor target for

Toni's bullets in case she followed unseen. When she came to the place where the sidewalk and wall branched west toward the sea, headlights spread around her.

What now? She turned. A hiss of air whizzed by her. She crouched. Toni and the gun did follow. By car. She could outrun Toni, but not Toni's car.

If she turned toward the sea, down the path to the Cliff House restaurant's lower observation deck, no car could follow. She turned and raced faster. A car door slammed. Footsteps sounded behind her. At the end of the path a three foot high wall protected ocean observers from the steep drop to the sea.

A small building shaped like a giant camera butted against the wall. It was the old camera obscura Angelo had mentioned on the radio. Fun loving tourists could view the ocean from inside it. Swell. She was running for her life, trapped against this camera obscura because she was grasping a tiny bowl depicting a camera obscura. The irony of it was no comfort.

A bullet cracked into the edge of the Giant Camera. With no other option, she scrambled over the wall and dropped to a very narrow ledge at the top of steep sea cliffs.

The red tide sparkled below the fog. Seals barked. Down was not an option. The rocks were too treacherous. Neither could she stay put like a sitting duck. All Toni would have to do was lean over the wall and fire.

Keeping her head lower than the wall and her left arm hugging the bowl, she used the fingers of her right hand to follow the wall as it curved around the observation deck while she half stumbled, half ran.

The end of the observation deck was as far as she

could go. There was no way to angle back to the street without meeting Toni. The only way forward was through clumps of high grass, mud, and sharp rocks down the hillside to the watery ruins of the Sutro Baths. Tiny ribbons of moonlight reflected silvery on the dark pools.

When she was a child, she played in the ruins of the former swimming pools, some still filled by water from underground springs. A rocky breakwater spanned the west side of the ruins, a barrier from the sea. On higher ground, the long wall of an Olympic-sized pool paralleled the sea level breakwater, ocean waves below it, dark spring water behind it.

In the dim light Mai could see only the gray cement of the wall's top, like a narrow bridge across deep space. She forced the bowl tightly against her side, sat on the uneven ground, and slid and slipped downward from grass clump to grass clump, trying to blend with the dark twists of the ground.

Midway down she came to a rock outcropping on which nothing grew and which sheered off in a steep drop. Before she could maneuver around it, the full moon swam out of the fog and she became a bright target.

Bullets sparked off the outcropping on both sides. Toni was not a practiced marksman. But Mai's heart was racing, her muscles cramping. She feared those random shots.

She had to get the bowl to safety. Clutching it to her side limited her mobility. She was scrambling down the steep slope with just one useful arm and it hurt like hell where Toni had smashed it with the rod. Fear knotted her stomach. She scooted and crawled awkwardly around the outcropping, aiming for the short grasses below it.

With screaming force a bullet dug violently into her left shoulder, blasted her onto her side. The bowl jolted from her arm, careened down the hillside, glinted once, twice, three times in the silver moonlight before plunging into the old swimming pool just up the hill from the breakwater.

The bowl itself reacted instantly to the water, glowing brightly. In a streak of light, a stream of fire, it cut through the dark water, hitting bottom in a blaze of red flashes.

Even as severe pain consumed her, Mai, barely able to breathe, her energy ebbing away, watched the oracle bowl as it flew off the cliff into the water. The bowl's strange light, its stream of fire, seemed normal to her, as if she expected it, as if it motioned to her.

The blood oozing warm down her back told her she was not dead yet. She gagged back the nausea which threatened to erupt in a retching cough and by willpower alone crawled down the hillside into the short grasses.

The bowl glowed under five feet of black water. Toni would see it, race around the Cliff House, and run down the broad tourist path to get it.

The moon spun above Mai. Her ears roared. She couldn't move without pain engulfing her. Toni's silhouette appeared at the top of the tourist path. Fighting as never before, watching both the eerie light from the bowl and Toni's shadow form, Mai forced herself the rest of the way down to the ruins. At the bottom of the hill she crawled onto the narrow bridge formed by the pool's side wall. Without thinking, she let her body fall into the pool's dark water.

The sudden surge of cold water snapped her teeth together, took what was left of her breath away. She stood on her toes in the water for what seemed centuries to catch her breath. The wind blew a current into the water. She felt she might float far, far away. She wanted to drift, face down, in the current.

The water was luminous. As if from a great distance, she noticed the fiery glow at the bottom of the pool. The oracle bowl. It was hers. She had to get it. Holding her breath, she dove forward until the fingers of one hand grazed its rim. She felt energy come to her from that touch. She closed her fingers around the rim.

Without knowing how, she held the bowl, lifted her head out of the water, and sidestroked to where a crumbling corner of an old maintenance building rose beside the pool. She knew the structure. She'd played in it. Recognizing the familiar walls, she summoned strength from her past, her childhood, her grandfather's strong arms. She managed to get out of the water, stand, and lean against the ruin, her dress dripping, cold and twisted against her legs.

She was aware of muffled footfalls in the sandy soil coming near the building. With a shaking hand she pushed the bowl securely into the elbow bend of her wounded arm and then, with a jerk, pulled the knife from its stiff leather sheath.

When she heard a crunch of grass at the corner of the building, she lurched out and bumped into Toni's shoulder. Her knife blade flashed in the moonlight. With not a lot of control she pressed its point under Toni's chin.

"Throw the gun as hard as you can, as far into the water as it will go, or the knife goes in as far as it will go," Mai said, steadying her voice by gritting her teeth.

When Mai heard the gun splash, she did not release the knife. "Enough. Enough of this, Toni. Too much sorrow over a bowl." It didn't sound too convincing. She took small breaths, unable to control the trembling in her hand. Toni flinched. Mai drew blood as the knife wavered across Toni's skin.

"Stop, Mai. Take it easy. You'll kill me."

Mai gripped the knife, steadied her hand, a little more in control because what Toni had just said terrified her. She almost had killed Toni earlier with the gun, now with the knife. Even if she could justify it, her grandfather would never forgive her for killing someone.

"No, I won't kill you." The knife tip etched a tiny jagged line down Toni's throat."

Toni cried out. "Okay. Okay. Mai, put the knife away."

Mai still did not pull the knife away. An idea was forming. She knew how to end this. "If I let you live, you do two things."

"Okay. Okay. Anything."

"First, you go straight to Edna." Mai took several deep breaths. "Tell Edna the bowl was looted like other things in her collection." Mai forced her voice, as well as her hand, to be steady. "You clean up Edna's collection. Return the stolen pieces. Destroy the fakes. Agree?"

"Agree."

Mai tightened the muscles in her legs. Stood stiller.

"Second, you give Attorney Chang names. You close down Conti's smuggling ring or Attorney Chang closes you down."

"All right. You win. Put down the knife."

Mai moved the knife tip to Toni's heart. "You go now. I'll be right behind you. I can throw this knife very accurately if you try anything."

Toni wasted no time. At street level she ran down the hill towards her studio.

It took Mai's last molecules of adrenalin to climb the high hill to her house, one foot in front of the other on the path which spun and lurched in rhythm with her stomach. Her body moved at tectonic plate speed. Her brain, however, motored on, urged her to make one last effort.

The steep hillside became the pine needles of her yard. She managed to hook the screen door handle with her fingers and pull it open. *Eek. Eek.* The rusted hinges yelled at her. She fell against the front door. Before her fingers could reach for the hidden key, the door opened.

Angelo caught her as she fell. "Jesus! What happened to you?" That was the last thing she heard. His arms supported her. That was the last thing she felt.

Two hours later, Mai lay propped against several pillows, her left shoulder and arm numb. She moved her legs slowly under the soft, warm blanket of her bed.

"The doctor says you'll live," Angelo said. "She dug a bullet out of your shoulder and she must have boiled you. You smelled rather alarming."

"Where's the bowl?"

"Downstairs in the false bottom of your kitchen cabinet, covered by a large mixing bowl and a small salad bowl. It's safe." He pulled her peacock necklace from his pocket. "And you'll need this tomorrow. I found it on my window sill."

"My mother's gift." She had forgotten it. Her mother's blessing returned. *May your life be filled with beauty always.* She'd have to work at that. "Would you just fasten it around my neck. I doubt I'll be able to lift my arms tomorrow." After Angelo had the clasp secured, Mai let her head fall against the pillows. "What are you doing here?"

"I was worried and came looking for you. It didn't help that the power was off when I got here. Your lights came on just before you fell through the door."

"It has been dark." She shifted a little. "I'm glad you came. You must have called the doctor."

"I called James. He sent her."

"She had a fit. Doesn't like the Wild West or bullet wounds. Or house calls." Mai closed her eyes. "I'm two seconds away from comatose. You must go home."

"I thought I'd better spend the night here."

"No." She was drifting off. "Go. Get ready for your extravaganza."

"If you're really all right."

His voice lingered in her head for a few more seconds. "Antibiotics and pain medication on the night stand," he said. "I'll lock everything downstairs."

She nodded but could only think *goodbye.*

SATURDAY

35

LOOKING EAST

Mai woke on Saturday morning and had to dress slowly even though she was anxious to get to Monterey to see her grandfather. Every part of her ached. She hoped Angelo had made it back in time to get everything ready for his project.

She couldn't drive. She called a friend to rescue her Jaguar from the wrong side of the street where she'd abandoned it and took a taxi to Monterey.

To hide her injuries, she wore a pale gold damask jacket embroidered with green bamboo and a green silk dress. The heavy cloth covered the tape and pads that wrapped her shoulder, and the sleeves of softer silk puffed out from shoulders to wrists, camouflaging all bangs and bruises.

She rubbed her hand across the delicate green bamboo on the gold silk which cloaked her wounds. She loved this jacket. It was a work of art. In her world, art cloaked many things.

Pain medicine helped.

At the hospital in Monterey she found her grandfather in a large private room on the first floor, in a white bed, part of his face covered with white bandages. Even though she knew the extent of his injury, her knees weakened seeing him so vulnerable. He had always been upright and sturdy for her. She pulled a chair to his bedside and took his hand.

"Grandfather, I'm here. I have the bowl."

A slight upturn of his lips and a gentle tightening of his fingers on her hand reassured her. Without moving his jaw much, he said, "I suppose you have a rather long story to tell me."

"Yes. And eventually you will have to listen to all of it. But not now. Can you open your eye?"

"Of course." After some effort, he did open it. "Ah. Yes. I can see you clearly." He took a breath. "You look so like your grandmother when she was your age."

That was a surprising thing to say. He never before had identified her with the past. She attributed it to the anesthetic but her hand automatically touched the peacock necklace, her mother's gift from the past.

"When you are well," she said, "we'll take the bowl to China."

He closed his eye. He lay silent. Mai thought he had fallen asleep. But after a minute, he said, "I believe I must allow destiny to take its course. It is natural that new generations replace the old. I held the bowl in my hands, studied it, and made drawings. I can never thank you enough for that." With a concentrated effort he opened his eye again. "But you know its song." His face and jaw were so still when he talked he seemed a ghost. "The bowl's history will always be mine. But now its future is yours."

Mai pinched her lips tight to prevent tears from flowing. Before she could speak, the doctor came in. "I'm sorry, Mai. You must let him sleep."

She kissed her grandfather's hand. "I'll come back this evening."

She listened to the doctor talk to her grandfather until she felt good enough to walk down the hall to the orthopedic ward to find Hunter. She owed him big time for apparently shooting Conti at the moment Conti fired at her grandfather.

During the cab ride from San Francisco she talked on the phone with James. He told her he suggested to the police that Conti, an international antiquity smuggler and suspected murderer, knew that Casa de Chang held items recovered by Interpol and he probably was attempting to steal back the Italian sorcerer's effigy of a naked lady which three days before Interpol had deprived him of. Hunter probably tracked the smuggler for Italy. The police would talk to Hunter and her grandfather but he felt sure the preliminary police report listed Conti's killing as probable self defense. Mai felt indebted to James. And, for the first time, she felt a strong connection to him. And to Hunter.

Hunter sat up straight in bed reading a magazine, his leg immobile in a very long cast. She tapped on the door and walked in. He looked her up and down slowly, then put the magazine on his lap and folded his hands across his chest. "Well, well. If it isn't little Mary Sunshine dressed all in gold. Have you come to thank me for saving your grandfather's life?"

"In your heavily sedated state, you may imagine

that to be the case, if you like." She picked up the magazine and leafed through it, feigning indifference.

He straightened the gown and pulled it farther down his bare leg, studying her face as he did so. "Wait a minute. Wait just one minute." He grabbed the magazine from her. "You found the bowl, didn't you? You have my bowl."

She smiled slightly, just enough not to gloat. "Medication often causes delusions. How many pain pills have you swallowed?"

"There aren't enough pills to make you bearable."

"Don't be too disappointed." She walked to the door. "There will be other relics that you can lose to me." He threw the magazine at her. She kept a straight face, put her hands together, and bowed. "Until we meet again."

Mai got into the taxi waiting for her, glad Hunter and her grandfather were in good hands and excited about Angelo's project.

All the streets adjacent to Custom House Plaza were closed to traffic. As close as the taxi could get Mai to Angelo's grand display was several blocks away at the opposite end of Alvarado.

As she headed down the street, sunlight glinted around her peacock necklace and shimmered off her golden jacket as her quick steps glided her towards the Plaza. The tape holding her together pulled her skin if she walked regularly.

Cypress, carrying a large arrangement of mustard blooms and eucalyptus twigs, came from behind her. "Cypress, are you coming to Angelo's installation?"

"Not me. I'm working. Bringing flowers to the Old Monterey Hotel."

"But you will come?"

"Too much hype over dumb draperies for my liking. I'll wait until he has a real art show. He can do better."

"But you'll walk down?"

"Maybe."

Cypress turned into the hotel and Mai followed a peanut cart with gigantic wheels down the center line of Alvarado past pink cotton candy spinning in shiny drums and an ice cream machine which swirled lemon sorbet into sugar cones. Helen Frye stood in line for a cone.

"Hello, Helen," Mai said. "I'm so glad you came."

"I had to force myself. Edna won't talk to me or the police."

Mai tried to sound neutral, although she was delighted that Edna would not be talking to the police. "Edna will do what she has to do. Give her time," Mai said.

"You're right, I suppose. Louis insisted I meet him here. Said it would be good for me. Help me quit worrying about the bowl. He asked me to dinner."

Now that was a curious pairing, Helen and Louis, uptight and fancy-free. Maybe Taoist wine was good for something after all.

"I hope you enjoy both the drapery and dinner," Mai said, and couldn't resist adding, "Drink some Taoist wine. It will be good for you too."

In Custom House Plaza *plein-air* artists had easels set up all around the Custom House. The gleaming, newly painted camera obscura was cordoned off so that the line of sight from it to the Custom House was free of spectators.

Angelo dashed up to Mai. His red silk shirt draped close against his body as if it were formed from molten bronze. He looked fabulous. He touched Mai's arms gently. "You look gorgeous. Are you all right?"

"Yes. Stuffed with pain pills. Are you ready?"

"The musicians are setting up in the Plaza garden. Will you help me with the camera obscura? I need a first class artist to explain it to the TV people."

"Of course."

The TV crew for "On Location with the Arts" had cameras rolling in front of the camera obscura. Robert Giles-Smyth talked into the microphone. "This is quite a day. We are here with thousands of others anxiously awaiting the draping of the historic Custom House." A fresh maroon carnation was in his lapel, his gray suit was spotless. Any tape or brace that might be on his ankle was hidden under a perfect pant leg. He showed absolutely no sign of yesterday's plunge from the Custom House scaffolding.

Angelo said to the publicity honcho, "If one of your cameramen will follow Mai Ling inside the camera obscura, you can film in there as well as out here. Both views will be breathtaking."

Mai and one cameraman stepped inside. "Stand there, by the canvas," Mai instructed. "Prepare yourself."

She pulled the door shut. Sunlight flashed through the hole. The Custom House splashed upside down in good focus on the white canvas and blue sky spilled across the floor.

"Holy smoke," the cameraman said. "Now that's magic."

Outside, Angelo stepped onto the small stage in front of the Custom House and raised both arms over his head. The crowd stopped moving. No one made a sound.

He lowered his arms. Several seconds ticked by. Then

very slowly, golden nylon unfurled and fell gracefully around the left two story wing. Minutes later, fabric covered the single story center section. The Custom House looked like a huge gold "L." Minutes went by. Nothing else happened. The crowd didn't move but it did mumble. Finally the right two story section became drapery and a golden "U" billowed in the breeze.

"Hurrah!" Cheers erupted from the crowd.

The ground crew quickly caught the weighted hem of the drapery and secured it tightly around the entire perimeter of the Custom House.

Atop the Custom House, a triangular jib ran up a line which stretched from the representational bowsprit on the right two story section to a mast raised on the left one. The corner of the jib was quickly secured to a cleat in the midsection railing. Two more jibs followed, each one on a line secured to a point higher on the mast than the previous one. As if waiting until all three jibs were ready, the wind picked up. The sails billowed dramatically.

"Bravo!" "Way to go!" "Yes!" The crowd shouted, hooted, clapped. Trumpets blared.

Inside the camera obscura, Mai stared at the golden Custom House. She saw what Angelo intended everyone to see, a symbolic merchant ship about to sail into a busy harbor laden with wealth. She hoped that viewers saw the same thing. That the merchant ship was upside down in the camera obscura about to sink would occur to no one but Angelo and she'd let him explain that later. He'd probably say, "View the world in a camera obscura and see the tentative nature of man's enterprises. Success today. Upside down tomorrow."

Mai slid open the door and stepped out of the dark

room into the noise and bright sun. The camera obscura and the golden drapery complemented each other, dark balanced by light. Sometimes, like today, she felt balanced. She shared both her grandfather's sorrow and Angelo's joy.

She looked at the crowd. It was a canvas of faces, vivid colors, hazy blurs. She put her hand on the warm wood of the camera obscura. Soon she would journey to China to return her ancestor's oracle bowl to a small temple somewhere on the Mountain of Flowing Water, wherever that was.

And she would take the bowl's song with her. If she kept its song playing in her head, the same melody would carry her through every crisis, every season, and always bring her around again to spring.

Today was a good day. She felt fine.

Far away from the noisy crowd, on Casa de Chang's high terrace, the peacock stood quite still, arched its iridescent blue neck, tossed its feathered crown, and enjoyed the gentle breath of wind through the cinnamon scented cassia trees in another garden on a different horizon.

ACKNOWLEDGEMENTS

I gathered information from a number of sources for this story. In particular, I relied on David Hockney's *Secret Knowledge* (London, 2001) to understand the camera obscura, and on Kerson and Rosemary Huang's *I Ching* (New York, 1985) whose translation and analysis of the Chinese classic clarified for me the role of the oracle in Chinese thought.

I am indebted to the following people who contributed both inspiration and practical assistance: publisher Jerry Simmons of INDI Publishing Group whose expertise and patience guided the production and distribution of the book; editor Mary Holden, whose corrections and enthusiastic suggestions improved the manuscript; author Carolyn Wheat and my fellow writers in her critique group, David Dooley, Suzanne Lowrie, John Mullen, and Cathy Worthingon, who helped me craft the scenes and structure; artists Justin Snow of BronzeArtwork in Escondido, California, and Tom Schrey of Artworks Foundry in Berkeley, California, who showed me the process of bronze casting; artist and teacher Jean Shen who brought the spirit of Chinese brush painting to me; Brian Weiner of The Illusion Factory in Woodland Hills, California, whose kind offer to help me in any way along the book production path I remembered often; and Melissa Jackson of The Original Pancake House who provided coffee and encouragement.

I am grateful to Leigh Weesner, my good friend, whose sense of humor put everything in proper perspective. And I am most grateful to Ted, my husband, who scouted locations with me on many occasions and whose support and encouragement I especially appreciate.

www.ingramcontent.com/pod-product-compliance
Lightning Source LLC
LaVergne TN
LVHW091033080826
845145LV00002B/474

* 9 7 8 1 9 3 5 6 3 6 0 2 1 *